THE ONLY GAME

A
HOME TEAM
NOVEL

THE
ONLY
GAME

MIKE
LUPICA

SIMON & SCHUSTER BOOKS FOR YOUNG READERS
NEW YORK LONDON TORONTO SYDNEY NEW DELHI

SIMON & SCHUSTER BOOKS FOR YOUNG READERS
An imprint of Simon & Schuster Children's Publishing Division
1230 Avenue of the Americas, New York, New York 10020
SIMON & SCHUSTER BOOKS FOR YOUNG READERS is a trademark of Simon & Schuster, Inc.
For information about special discounts for bulk purchases, please contact Simon & Schuster
Special Sales at 1-866-506-1949 or business@simonandschuster.com.
The Simon & Schuster Speakers Bureau can bring authors to your live event. For more
information or to book an event, contact the Simon & Schuster Speakers Bureau at
1-866-248-3049 or visit our website at www.simonspeakers.com.
Book design by Lucy Ruth Cummins
The text for this book is set in Adobe Garamond Pro.
Manufactured in the United States of America
1214 FFG
2 4 6 8 10 9 7 5 3 1
Library of Congress Cataloging-in-Publication Data
Lupica, Mike.
The only game / Mike Lupica.
pages cm
"A Home Team Novel."
Summary: Sixth grade is supposed to be the year that Jack Callahan
would lead his team to a record-shattering season and the Little League
World Series, but after the death of his brother he loses interest in baseball and
only Cassie, star of the girls' softball team, seems to understand.
ISBN 978-1-4814-0995-7 (hardcover : alk. paper) — ISBN 978-1-4814-0997-1 (eBook)
[1. Baseball—Fiction. 2. Grief—Fiction. 3. Friendship—Fiction. 4. Bullies—Fiction.] I. Title.
PZ7.L97914Onl 2015
[Fic]—dc23   2014015989

FIRST
EDITION

For Christopher and Alex and Zach and Hannah

Acknowledgments

This book is written in the spirit of every boy and girl
I have ever coached, all the ones who had their own dreams,
and taught me a lot more than I taught them.

ONE

After what had been the longest year of Jack Callahan's life, it was baseball season again.

It had always been the best season for him. It was like Christmas came in the spring and lasted all the way through summer.

It was the first official day of baseball at Highland Park, the real center of town in Walton. The center of town and the center of baseball in the town. They had four Little League fields, all of them looking brand-new, as if the grass had been painted a perfect green and the dirt had been brought here from the big leagues for the batting box and pitcher's mound and base paths. Even the white numbers set against the dark blue of the outfield walls looked as if they had been painted that morning.

From the time he'd been old enough to play Little League, after he'd moved up from T-ball, this field or the one next to it or the two at the other end of Highland Park had felt like Jack's home away from home.

Always, no matter what else was going on, he'd felt happy here, and safe.

Safe at home.

When they'd arrived at the field, he'd pointed out to his best friend, Gus Morales, how new everything looked, and Gus had said, "Yeah, because the first day of baseball never gets old."

Gus's family had come to the United States from Santo Domingo in the Dominican Republic when Gus—full name Gustavo Alberto Morales—was still a baby. Gus had always told Jack that baseball in the Dominican was even more serious than Jack had read or heard. Baseball was like the national religion of Gus's country, and a really good ball field, like the ball fields at Highland Park, was like church.

Gus told stories that his father had told him: stories about being so poor when he was a boy that he'd played ball in abandoned lots or in the street, using broom handles for bats and old milk cartons for gloves.

Maybe that was why Gus loved baseball as much as he did. Just not as much as Jack did. And as good a player as Gus was, a big first baseman with power, a lefty hitter and lefty thrower who could field as well as he could hit, he wasn't as good as Jack Callahan.

Jack was the best seventh grader in town, the best pitcher and the best shortstop when he wasn't pitching. He'd have been the best outfielder if his coaches had ever needed him to play out there. There were two leagues at the sixth-grade/seventh-grade level in Walton, one called the Atlantic and one called the Pacific. The best kids went to the Atlantic each year. Back in February, tryouts had been held in the gym at Walton High School. The gym was filled with baseball that day, even though it was still winter. Jack had graded higher than any other kid in town his age.

Again.

Nobody was supposed to know the scores, but by the time they all left the gym that day, everybody knew his.

"Shocker, you scoring like that," Gus had said. "For you baseball's like this test where you already know the answers."

The next week he was the first player drafted when the coaches held their draft.

"Another shocker," Gus said at the time.

"You know I don't care about any of that stuff," Jack had said. "I'm just glad you were still around when our team picked again."

The start of the season seemed so far away to Jack then, with snow still on the ground outside, Jack thinking about the baseball season the way he always had.

Gus had said, "If another team had picked me, I would have demanded a trade. Dude, we're the team."

Their team was the Rays this season. Last season they were sixth graders and good enough to play in the Atlantic division. They'd been on the Red Sox and had rolled through the league, losing just one game before they lost in the finals by a run, bottom of the last inning.

And this year the stakes had been raised, this year was their shot at the Little League World Series in Williamsport, Pennsylvania. The way it worked in Walton was they sent two teams every year into the County All-Star League; one was the winner of the Atlantic, and the other a team made up of the best players from the rest of the division.

Then the winner of the County All-Star League was the one that punched its ticket into the tournament that finally put you into the World Series if you kept winning through your region and your state.

Gus was already obsessed—totally—with the chance that he

might not only get to Williamsport, but play baseball on national television, because ESPN had been televising the Little League World Series since before they were both born.

"You know the team everybody's going to want to watch this summer?" Gus was saying now at Highland Park. "Ours." Then he put out his right hand to Jack and started one of those complicated fist bumps and handshakes and arm moves—everything except a couple of dance steps—that were sometimes more complicated to Jack than seventh-grade algebra.

"You think there are cameras on you even when they're not," Jack said.

"Exactly!" Gus said. "That way, when the real cameras are on me, I'll be ready."

"Can't wait."

"You'll be right there with me," Gus said, "because you're like my ticket to it all."

For now, a long way from Gus's dream, Jack took in the scene all around them: first official day of practice, all the players on the field for the first time, players from some of the other teams in their league on the three other fields.

Jack Callahan: back out there with Gus and the rest of the guys, taking it all in, baseball and him back together.

Wanting to love it even more than he ever had before.

When they took the field, he ran out to shortstop, Gus was

at first, Brett Hawkins—known as Hawk—at third base, T. W. Stanley at second, Scott Sutter at catcher. Coach John Leonard stood next to Scott at home plate, hitting ground balls, chattering away like he was as excited as any of the players on his team to be out here today, at least as excited as his own son, Gregg, out in center field.

All this baseball, between the green grass and the blue sky.

"Guy I heard on TV one time, some sportswriter, called baseball the greatest game ever invented by mortal minds," Coach said, then slapped a hard grounder to Jack's left, toward the middle of the diamond.

Jack didn't hurry. The parents who'd watched him grow up in baseball, especially the ones who'd played ball themselves, talked about how he never rushed himself, even on the toughest plays. How sometimes he seemed to be moving to the ball before the ball was even hit.

And how once he was in motion, it was as if he was gliding.

So Jack was gliding to the ball now that they were on the field and in the middle of infield drills. He moved to his left after a ground ball up the middle, almost as if he knew where it was going to end up better than it did. He cut the ball off in front of the second-base bag, reached down, and felt the ball in the pocket of his Dustin Pedroia glove, the one he'd broken in perfectly by the end of last season.

Not even breaking stride as he kept moving to his left, to the rightfield side of second now, making the transition of glove to bare hand, his eyes picking up Gus at first base even though Jack knew he could make a play like this blindfolded. He whipped a perfect sidearm throw to Gus, perfect strike.

"Yeah!" Gus yelled, smiling at Jack, pointing with his glove, like he wasn't just the happiest kid at Highland Park in that moment, but the happiest kid in the whole town.

Jack pointed back at him and ran back to short as Coach hit the next grounder to T. W. Stanley.

Jack took off his cap, the same blue as the one the Tampa Bay Rays wore, the logo exactly right. He used the cap to wipe some sweat off his forehead, even though his teammates said they never saw him sweat. Even though the caps they were wearing were adjustable, they still looked exactly like the ones the real Rays wore. No surprise there. They did things right in Walton when it came to baseball.

Oh, the other sports were big here too, for boys and girls. Jack and Gus played football and basketball together, and the soccer program in town was huge. So was the lacrosse program, one that took away kids that Jack knew would have been awesome in baseball. Jack's father explained it by saying that the best lacrosse players in high school could usually punch their own ticket to the best colleges, and their parents wanted to get them started on that road as early as possible.

"You think they love lacrosse the way I love baseball?" he'd asked his dad one time last season.

His dad had smiled and said, "The only love greater than that is the one I have for you, kid."

More than anything, Walton was a baseball town, in a baseball region, in a baseball state. Now, because their team looked even more loaded than it did last season, baseball in Walton felt bigger than it ever had. Everyone was dreaming about making it to Williamsport and the World Series.

It just seemed that the guys around Jack on this field were dreaming a little bigger and a little harder, starting with Gus Morales.

This season was going to be the one they would talk about for the rest of their lives. Gus had been saying that for weeks, from the time their team was set and they knew John Leonard was going to be their coach. Gus knew they were going to have the best team of kids their age anywhere in the state or in the region or in the country.

"Why stop there?" Jack said. "Why not the greatest team of twelve-year-olds in the history of the planet Earth?"

"Go ahead, mock me."

"If you insist," Jack said.

This was when they had been stretching in the outfield grass, more to feel the grass under them than for the stretching. Gus talked about how he'd been waiting for this day since they'd lost to Cortland Lakes.

Jack knew Gus Morales had great parents, a great sister, a great life being a kid in Walton. But the good life to him meant baseball, green grass underneath him and the sun high in the sky, two more hours of practice ahead of him, the whole season after that. To him, that was living.

Gus always liked to say that he wanted to be as good as Jack, having no idea—none—how much Jack wanted to be him today.

His friend, born in the Dominican and born to a love of the game, to whom none of this got old, Gus with his new first baseman's mitt and his new cleats and his new blue batting gloves.

Jack had tried to stop his parents from spending as much as they had on new cleats for him—Michael Jordan kids' cleats—and spending as much as they had on a new bat, way too much on the bat, a yellow-and-black Easton S1. But there was no stopping either one of them; they were on a mission. Jack's mom said last year's spikes were too small. His dad said you needed a new bat every year as you got bigger and your swing speed increased. That was just common sense.

"Besides," Jack's dad said, "if you're going to have the

best season of your life, you need the best equipment. Case closed."

It was as if, Jack thought, his parents thought they'd be playing the season right along with him. Like they wanted this season to be as great as Gus was sure it was going to be.

"Hey!" It was Coach Leonard, calling out to Jack from the batter's box, ball in his left hand, bat on his shoulder, ready to go. "Is my shortstop's head in the game, or is he staring into outer space?"

"Sorry, Coach," Jack said. "You got me. I zoned out there for a second."

Coach Leonard was smiling. "Season already starting to drag a little bit for you, Jack?"

"Little bit," Jack said.

The guys around him in the infield laughed.

They worked on double plays for a little while then, starting to read one another a little better with each play, timing their throws just right. Jack took one underhand throw from T.W. that was too high at second, high and wide to the third-base side of the bag. But Jack reached up with his bare hand, not breaking stride or losing where the bag was, making the catch and the throw to Gus in one graceful motion.

And heard T.W. behind him say, "You should be playing for the real Rays."

Jack slapped him lightly on the shoulder with his glove as he headed back to shortstop. "You just gave me a wide-right throw to make me look good," he said.

"I wish," T.W. said.

T.W. came over and stood next to Jack while Hawk fielded bunts. "You okay?" he said.

"I'm good."

"Okay to ask?"

Jack slapped him again with his glove and said, "Yeah, it's okay. We're teammates, aren't we?"

Before long it was time for their first batting practice of the season. Coach Leonard said he hadn't set the whole batting order in his mind yet. But he said that he wanted the first four hitters today to be the four he thought he was going to put at the top of the order when the season started:

T.W.

Gregg.

Jack.

Gus.

Coach Leonard pitched, from behind the mound. "Stay loose, boys," he said. "I've got a lot more arm than an old man is supposed to have." When it was Jack's turn to hit, he walked to the plate with his new Easton in his hands—no batting gloves for him, not one time since he'd started playing organized ball. He wanted to feel the bat, and he was now, swinging like it was the middle of the season already.

He pulled the first pitch he saw, hard down the leftfield line. Line drive over second next, T.W. saying it sounded like a police siren going past him. Then Jack pounded one up the gap in right-center, the ball rolling all the way to the wall.

He told himself he might as well make these swings count.

His next swing put the ball over the leftfield fence.

Jack finished by dropping a perfect bunt down the third-base line, running it out like he was trying to beat the ball out in a game. Then he moved around the bases while Gus took his swings. When he got back to the bench, he grabbed his Pedroia glove, took off his batting helmet, and ran out to short.

Now he told himself not to lose focus, not this close to the end.

There was all this chatter while the rest of the guys hit. All of what his dad called the music of baseball. Jack's dad, who'd been a star shortstop himself at Walton High School, then a good enough prospect later that he was drafted by the Red Sox out of Boston College before he decided to go to law school instead.

"But you've got all those trophies in your office," Jack had said the first time his dad told him he knew he wasn't good enough to ever make it to the big leagues. "And you say you loved it the way I do."

And his dad had put his arm around him that day and said, "Sometimes it's about more than the love of the game."

Jack remembered that now, for the first time in a long time, as if it had happened yesterday.

They finished practice with some situational drills, guys taking their infield and outfield positions, other guys running the bases, some cutoff plays. Guys tried to score from second base on balls Coach Leonard would hit in front of the outfielders.

When they were done for the day, Coach gathered the players around him in the grass behind shortstop, telling them he knew they had high expectations for themselves this season and that he was cool with that.

"But here's my biggest hope," he said. "That by the end of the season every one of you will be a better baseball player than he is right now."

Some of the other guys, the ones whose parents hadn't shown up yet, went back to the outfield to throw the ball around, goof around, throw high fly balls. Gregg Leonard got whoops when he caught one behind his back.

Jack's mom had told him she might be a little late; she had to stop and do some shopping for dinner.

Good, Jack thought.

Eventually the last two players on the field were Gregg Leonard, the leftfielder, and Andre Williams, who was going to be one of the starting pitchers. They were running races around the bases, timing each other with the stopwatches on their phones.

Now or never, Jack told himself.

Coach was at the end of the bench, tossing batting helmets into a duffel bag.

Jack took one last look around: his boys running the bases, the advertisements for town businesses across the outfield walls, the outfield grass, still remembering the way the ball had felt coming off his bat when he had hit his shot over the leftfield fence in batting practice.

It was official, on the first official day: He loved baseball more than he ever had.

Jack put his bat and glove and cap into his new bat bag now, took a deep breath, walked over to Coach, and told him he was quitting the team.

TWO

He waited until both his parents were there at dinner, his dad home from work, before telling them what he'd told Coach Leonard, knowing he couldn't put it off any longer. Just the thought of having to do it made him imagine his day as being more wrecked than it already was.

This was after the short ride home in the car with his mom from Highland Park—Jack walked to the fields sometimes, or rode his bike—when he seemed more quiet than usual.

Just not as quiet as things got at the table when he told them.

"You can't possibly be serious," his mom said.

That was after she had opened and closed her mouth a couple of times, as if waiting for the right words to come out of it.

"I am serious, Mom."

"You are quitting baseball?" his dad said. "No, you're not."

Not making it sound like an order, like he was telling Jack he had to play baseball or else. It was more like him saying he didn't believe what Jack was telling him.

"You're gonna to have to explain this to me," his dad said. "To both of us."

"Not sure I can."

"Try," his mother said. "You can't do something like this without a good reason."

"Basically I just don't feel like playing right now," he said.

"No," she said.

Jack looked back at her. "You don't believe me?"

"What I don't believe is what I'm hearing from across this table."

Tim Callahan, his dad, tried to take the lead. "You made a decision like this—and you didn't even run it by us?"

"Maybe it was because I knew how you'd react," Jack said. "Pretty much the way you're reacting right now."

His mom tried to stay cool, but Jack could see the effort it was taking. "This isn't about our reaction," she said. "It's about your decision. One you still haven't explained very well, I'm afraid."

"My heart's not in it, that's my explanation," Jack said. "And haven't you guys always told me that playing sports is supposed to be up to me?"

"Looks like you've taken it a step further now," his dad said, "and decided that also applies to not playing, apparently."

Jack nodded, looking at the food left on his plate, the hamburger and fries he'd barely touched.

Gail Callahan said, "But you love baseball, sweetheart. I always hear you and Gus talking about how you might make it all the way to the Little League World Series this year."

Jack knew how much she loved him, how much she loved watching him play ball. She talked about that all the time, how it was Jack who'd made her a baseball fan, for the first time in her life.

Jack also knew this: how much he was going to be letting her down by quitting the Rays, along with letting down everybody else who mattered to him.

"Have you told Gus yet?" his dad said.

"No," Jack said. "I told Coach and now I'm telling you guys. I'm gonna call Gus after we finish dinner. I told Coach not to say anything to the rest of the guys. I guess I'll have to face them at practice tomorrow."

"Plus, you could change your mind by tomorrow," his mom said, still sounding hopeful that might happen.

"I'm not changing my mind, Mom."

She said, "About the sport you're best at?"

"This all started with me knowing that I'm just not ready," Jack said. "You can at least get that, right?"

"I'm trying to," his dad said. "But what I don't get is how you were ready for football, and then basketball after that. I thought if you were going to take a season off, it would've been football, that being so close . . ."

His dad's voice drifted away now, the way it did when they got anywhere near talking about last summer.

"I just thought baseball would be so great for all of us," his mom said. "You have no idea how much your father and I were looking forward to watching you play."

"I do have an idea," Jack said. "But I have to play for me."

She said, "We've been waiting . . . all year to be back at those fields."

Jack looked at her. "You mean so things could be the way they used to be?"

He was sorry as soon as his words were in the air between them, even before he saw the hurt look on her face.

"You know I didn't mean it that way," she said.

"I know, Mom. I'm sorry, I sound like an idiot sometimes."

"You've never been an idiot for one single day," she said.

"Listen, you guys, I already feel like I'm letting the team down. I don't want to feel like I'm letting you down too."

"You've never let us down either," his dad said. "You've been more of a champ over the past year than you've ever been in sports. You know how proud your mother and I are."

"I know you think you've thought this through," his mom said. "But maybe this is a good thing, the talk we're having right now, the three of us talking it through together."

"Not if you think I'm changing my mind," Jack said.

There was another long silence now at the table. Jack was used to that kind of silence by now, at this table, in their house, in his life.

"I might stop playing baseball for good," he said.

"You don't mean that," his dad said.

"I do."

"You can't."

"Maybe it's time to try something else for a change, start all over," he said. "A lot of my friends think I'd be great at lacrosse."

His dad said, "You're a ballplayer."

"If I don't feel like one," Jack said, "then I'm not one."

He had thought about not trying out at all, back in February.

Now he wished he hadn't, because it would've all been over now, long over. Gus would know, the whole baseball town of Walton would know.

But he had to be sure he was doing the right thing. Today had convinced him that he was.

His dad said, "You know we're not going to pressure you to do something you don't want to."

"I know."

"We trust you, Jack," his mom said. "You know that, don't you? We trust you even when we don't agree with you."

He nodded again.

"But what I'm worried about mostly is all the free time you're going to have on your hands," she said. "And it will be free time apart from your best friends. I still think the best thing, for all of us, is to keep busy."

"I've been keeping pretty busy, Mom."

"Not saying you haven't. But when your dad talked about not putting pressure on yourself . . . don't you think that because of the player you are, you're putting more pressure on yourself by not playing?"

Jack said, "You think I haven't thought about that?"

He shook his head now, hard, and said, "I'm just not ready."

"How about you do this?" his dad said. "How about I call Coach and tell him you want a couple of days to just think this through? A week even. Just to make sure that you're sure."

It just came out of Jack then, because he couldn't help himself. This wasn't the night to avoid the subject.

"Baseball won't bring my brother back," he said, knowing his voice was way too loud.

Then he asked to be excused.

THREE

His brother Brad, full name Bradley Jackson Callahan, had died in August of the previous summer, riding dirt bikes with his friends one night in an empty field next to Walton Country Club, part of the land that was going to make up a new nine holes for the club.

It wasn't dark yet when it happened. Brad and his boys were riding in that gray time between day and night when you had to stop playing ball, because you could no longer see the ball.

They had never ridden their bikes there before. There were NO TRESPASSING signs all over the place.

But those had never stopped Brad Callahan. He always thought the "no" in any sign meant no for everybody else and "no problem" for him.

"You know me, little bro," he'd say to Jack. "I'm like those guys in *Top Gun*."

It was one of Brad's all-time favorite old movies, and Jack would always know what was coming next, but he'd just wait for it.

"I feel the need for speed!" his brother would yell.

It wasn't even Brad's own bike. He didn't have one of his own—he hadn't even turned sixteen yet. The one he was riding belonged to his friend Spence, who was sixteen the night it happened and had a garage full of dirt bikes. Spence's family had a lot of money, and he already was driving around Walton in the brand-new car he'd gotten as soon as he got his driver's license.

Brad had always hung around with older kids.

Spence and the other two guys riding that night said Brad never saw the drop coming, because of the sketchy light; the color of the ground was the color of the sky, everything blending together. But Brad was the one in the lead, of course. He had to be first, like life was one big race. Jack went one time to see where it had happened. The drop was so steep he imagined his brother having gone over a cliff.

"The lead dog," Brad had called himself.

He was going too fast. Of course he was going too fast. Then suddenly he was flying into space. Jack imagined him chasing the night and finally catching it. Somehow the other boys stopped in time, their bikes skidding on their sides.

Not Brad.

The police and the doctors on the scene said that when he landed at the base of the tree, it was the same as if he'd hit that tree with a speeding car.

A month away from his sixteenth birthday, Jack's older brother was gone. He had always been a risk taker. He kept getting into trouble for that, for being Brad. He'd come home sometimes and race upstairs—going fast even when he was only racing against himself—and brag to Jack about taking his skateboard into town and holding on to the back of a bus, until a town cop spotted him one day and brought him home in a blue-and-white Walton Police Department car, and Brad ended up grounded for a solid month.

Grounded again.

That night Jack said to his brother, "Was it worth it?"

And Brad had said, "Oh yeah."

Jack said, "Mom and Dad were really mad this time."

"Can't help myself, little bro. I'm always gonna be that guy."

"What guy?"

"The guy having too much fun."

"I heard Dad from up here telling you that you can have too much fun sometimes."

"Not possible, little bro. Not possible."

Until too much fun got him killed a few weeks before he was supposed to start tenth grade.

He'd never been as good as Jack in sports, any sport, certainly not baseball. Maybe that was why Brad kept making up his own sports, his own competitions, on water skis or Jet Skis or surfing or snowboarding in the winter. Jack had always thought of his big brother as one of those freestyle skiers on ESPN's X Games. One of those crazy high-flying dudes.

It was their dad who had taught Jack baseball, Jack thinking it was almost like he'd inherited the right genes and right temperament and right attitude from his dad. Brad hadn't. "Too slow," he'd say. "Too boring. The games go way too long." Still, somehow Brad always found time to play ball with Jack when their dad was working, or traveling.

He'd find ways to make baseball even more fun for his little bro—he always called Jack that, even though by last summer they were practically the same height—as if he liked baseball more in the backyard with Jack than he liked any other games.

Brad had quit playing games for real after Little League.

"The only difference between us that I can see," Brad would tell Jack, "is that you're crazy about baseball and I'm just plain old crazy."

So Jack played baseball and his other old-school sports and never got into trouble. Brad was always getting into—and out of—trouble, mostly because nobody, starting with their parents, could ever stay mad at Brad Callahan for long.

It wasn't just the fun in him, their mom would say. It was all the life in him.

Only now he was dead. All that fun taken out of their family, out of their lives, for good.

Jack went upstairs to his bedroom, past the closed door to Brad's old room, and turned on the TV set he was allowed to have in there now to watch Monday Night Baseball on ESPN, Red Sox against the Orioles. He always liked watching Pedroia play, just because he did everything in baseball, the little things and the big things, exactly right.

Jack had gotten the new flat-screen TV at the beginning of the school year. Even at twelve, he was smart enough to see what was happening now that Brad was gone: This was going to be the year of getting stuff.

And it was more than that—it was the year of his mom

worrying about him more than she ever had before his brother's accident, just about every time he went out of the house. Jack could see her trying to be casual about it. But even when he'd ride his bike the few blocks to Highland Park, or the few blocks to Gus's house in the other direction, she'd say something like, "Hey, shoot me a text when you get there, big guy."

One time Jack had said, "Maybe you should put one of those tracking devices on me, Mom."

And she'd grinned and said, "Okay."

He kept waiting for his mom now, sure the bedroom door was going to open any minute, either she or his dad wanting to talk a little more about him quitting the Rays.

They surprised him this time. The door didn't open. Maybe they were both going to be cool about his decision. They were cool, his mom and dad, despite what had happened to them; to all of them.

They were trying to do something that Jack, even at his age, knew was impossible: make their world back into what it was before Brad snuck off and went dirt-biking that night.

It was eight thirty now.

Jack knew he couldn't put off calling Gus any longer.

So he punched out his number.

"What's good?" Gus said when he answered.

"You," Jack said.

The way they began all their phone conversations.

"Not as good as you," Gus said.

Because he always said that.

"Actually," Jack said, "I gotta tell you something that is not good. That stinks."

Before he lost his nerve, he told Gus what he'd told Coach, and what he'd told his parents at dinner.

Told his best friend he was quitting the team.

Gus didn't say anything at first, maybe the longest he'd ever gone without talking in any conversation, to the point where Jack started to think his best friend had hung up on him.

But finally Gus said, "Are you joking?"

"It's no joke, trust me."

"You can't do this to me. You can't do this to us."

"I have to."

"You're too good. We're too good. Not just the Rays. You and me. We're a team, remember?"

Jack closed his eyes. He'd known Gus wouldn't make things easy for him.

"Gus, it's like I told Coach—"

"Is this about your brother?"

"It's not about any one thing."

It was as if Gus hadn't heard him. "This is because of your brother now?"

Gus never talked around things. It was one of the things Jack loved about him: He came right at you.

"I don't know," Jack said. "Maybe."

"C'mon, dude. Maybe's not good enough, not for something this important."

"Maybe it was always more important to you than it was to me."

"No way," Gus said. "No way. All we've been talking about for the past two years is what it was gonna be like when we were twelve. How many nights did we watch the Little League World Series on television and you'd say, 'Someday that's gonna be us.' Well, this is someday. This is the year. Not my year. Our year."

"It's still your year," Jack said. "Even if the Rays don't win, you'll get picked for All-Stars, no problem, and you can still end up in Williamsport."

"I don't want to do it without you."

"You're gonna have to."

In a quiet voice Jack could barely hear, Gus said, "You're my best friend. Please don't do this to me."

"You make it sound like I'm leaving town," Jack said.

"It's gonna feel that way."

"Gus, you know I'm still gonna be your friend."

Gus paused again, then said, "This is your idea of being my friend?"

"Gus, this isn't about you."

He laughed. "Now you *are* joking. Of course it's about me."

Jack heard him laugh then, as if trying to make things the way they usually were between them, not like they had been tonight. Like it was the old Jack and the old Gus. "Isn't everything about me?" Gus said.

Then he said again, "Don't do this."

"Don't make this harder than it already is."

"What, you want me to make it easy for you? You drop this on me without even talking to me about it and now you want me to feel sorry for you? Well, sor-ry."

Jack said, "I'm just not feeling it right now with baseball. I can't explain it any better than that."

"I saw you on that field today," Gus said. "I know you've always been listening to me when I told you what baseball was like in the Dominican for my father and his friends. Most people don't understand. You always understood."

"This isn't about that."

Gus Morales didn't let things go, ever. He said, "And nobody understands you better than I do. I saw you on that field. And you were feeling it."

Jack said, "I was faking it," knowing how small his voice must sound in that moment. As small as he felt.

He waited for Gus to say something else.

Finally Jack said, "Gus? You still there?"

He wasn't. Jack was talking to himself by then. He'd been doing that a lot lately, just not out loud.

He knew how much he was going to miss baseball. He was missing it already, just watching the Red Sox play the Orioles on television. Now he wondered how much he was going to have to miss his best friend, too.

But maybe you could get better at missing things—and people—with enough practice.

FOUR

The next day at school, the girl saved him.

At least Gus had spared Jack the trouble of telling the team himself; by the time Jack got to the cafeteria for lunch, it wasn't just the guys on the team who knew Jack had quit—it seemed like the whole school knew.

And maybe the whole town.

Jack could tell that no one else wanted to rough him up about his decision the way Gus had on the phone, whether they liked it or not. But that was the way it had been the whole school year, everybody careful with what they said to Jack because of Brad. Everybody careful with how they treated him, mostly his friends talking around what had happened to his brother, afraid that something might come out wrong.

There were times during the school year when Jack had thought, *They treat me like I'm sick.*

Gus hadn't ignored him completely when Jack got to school. But he was still mad and making no attempt to hide it. Not that it would have done any good. Gus was worse at hiding his feelings than he was at ice skating.

Before their first class together, English, Jack had said, "You want to talk about this?"

"Nothing more to say," Gus said. "Like you told me last night. If you don't trust me enough to tell me what's really going on, nope, nothing more to say."

Then he sat down.

T.W. Stanley came up to Jack after English—they had lockers next to each other—and said, "Guess it's really true, huh?"

"Yeah."

"Dude," T.W. said. "I am so sorry."

"Just taking the season off," Jack said.

"Well, yeah," T.W. said, "but it's, like, your season."

Before the morning was out, Jack had talked about it with

Andre, and Scott Sutter, and Jerry York, the rightfielder for the Rays who was also going to be the team's closer. He could tell they were all holding back; all wanted more of an explanation.

But nobody pressed him, and not just because he was the kid who'd lost his brother last summer. Jack knew it was more than that.

It was because in their minds he was still the star of the team, and for as long as he could remember, he'd gotten star treatment from the other kids even though he'd never asked for it and didn't want it. That wasn't why he loved being a part of the teams he'd played on, in any sport. He loved being on teams—he didn't have to be *the* guy, because he loved being one of the guys.

But he didn't feel like one of the guys today.

Gus didn't sit with Jack for the first time the whole school year, or the one before that, or as far back as Jack could remember. He sat across the room with Gregg Leonard and Hawk, and even though Jack knew he should go over there, not let things get any worse than they were already, he just got the feeling that he wasn't welcome.

So Jack took his tray and sat at the end of a long table with a bunch of girls at the other end, one of them Cassie Bennett, as much a star of the girls' softball team in Walton as Jack was the star of the Rays.

Until yesterday, anyway.

MIKE LUPICA

Next to Jack was a boy named Teddy, whom Jack liked even though he didn't know him all that well, probably because Teddy wasn't much of an athlete. Teddy Madden was the overweight kid in the seventh grade the kids called Teddy Bear, and a lot of other things behind his back.

And not always behind his back.

Maybe that was why Jack would find himself looking out for Teddy in gym class when he thought some of the other guys crossed the line, even though they said they were just kidding around. Jack knew that sometimes you couldn't pick and choose the things you didn't like about your life. The things that hurt you, whether it was being too heavy, or something a lot worse than that.

Teddy didn't bring up baseball at lunch. They just talked with another guy named Jerry about school stuff, starting with an algebra quiz that had been sprung on them right before lunch. It had been as much of a disaster for Teddy as it had been for Jack.

Mr. Kahn was their algebra teacher. Teddy kept calling him "Genghis Kahn" at the table. Jerry finally asked who Genghis Kahn was.

Teddy, who could be really funny when you gave him the chance, looked at Jack and said, "Told you I was the only one listening in history."

"Little help here, guy," Jerry said. "That doesn't tell me who this Genghis guy was."

Teddy grinned. "Meanest khan in the world until our Mr. Kahn."

Suddenly Gus was at the table.

"You've never been a quitter in your life," he said to Jack. "You can't turn into one now."

He was talking loudly.

"I'm not a quitter," Jack said, keeping his own voice low. "You know that better than anyone."

"I thought I knew you," Gus said. "Guess I was wrong."

"That's wrong," Jack said. "And this isn't the right place for this."

Gus ignored him.

"This isn't just about you," he said. "It's about me and Gregg and Hawk and all the other guys on the team."

He wasn't lowering his voice even a little bit. Jack could see past Gus now, could see kids at other tables staring, watching a show Jack didn't want to be a part of.

"What you're doing affects the rest of us," Gus said. "And that's not fair."

Jack was about to tell him that a lot of things in life weren't fair. But he didn't. That wasn't something you said to a friend, and Gus was his friend, even if he wasn't acting much like one right now.

"Are you coming to practice today or not?" Gus said. "And I mean to play."

Now there was a voice louder than Gus Morales's—much—from the other end of the table.

"How dense are you, Morales?"

Jack turned, they all turned, and saw Cassie Bennett, standing now, hands on hips, eyes on fire. Maybe her hair was about to be on fire too.

"He's not playing," she said. "What part of that aren't you getting?"

"I wasn't talking to you, Cassie," Gus said.

But with a lot less attitude than he'd been giving to Jack.

"Well, you're talking to me now," Cassie said. "The conversation is over, lunch is over, move on."

Jack stared at her, amazed at what was happening, how fast it had all happened. He saw Gus's twin sister Angela, Cassie's best friend and one of her teammates on the softball team, staring at Cassie too, eyes big. Angela and Gus were fraternal twins, not identical. But they looked identical enough to Jack.

"This has nothing to do with you," Gus said, but the fight was going out of him now, because of who he was up against. Nobody in the seventh grade wanted to tangle with Cassie Bennett.

Boy or girl.

"Are you serious?" she said now. "You and your big mouth

have made it about everybody in the room, and maybe upstairs in the teachers' lounge."

The bell rang then, sounding to Jack like the bell you'd hear ending a round in the prizefights he watched with his grandfather sometimes.

Gus started to say one last thing to Jack but didn't. He just shook his head and walked away.

Cassie walked down to Jack, leaned over, and said, "If you don't want to play, don't play," and went out the double doors, heading for her one o'clock class.

Teddy watched her go the way Jack did, until she was down the hall and out of sight.

"You know all those books and movies where kids end up battling to save all of mankind?" Teddy said. "Well, if we ever end up in that situation and have to pick our team, I'm choosing Cassie first."

"I hear you," Jack said.

FIVE

Jack was walking home from school that day, having cleared it with his mom before he'd left the house in the morning. He had this feeling he'd want to be alone later.

Now he was sure of it.

He was tired of answering questions, feeling almost like he'd been on trial since he'd told Coach he was leaving the team after just one practice. He wished now that he hadn't even gone to tryouts, hadn't made Coach waste his first pick on him. But back in February he hadn't decided what he was going to do—what he had to do.

Jack knew there was a part of him wanting to tell everybody, even the ones on the team who said they understood, or that they respected his decision even if they didn't understand, how they were missing the point. But he knew there was no sense in doing that. It wasn't going to change his situation, or theirs.

He was going to do what Brad used to talk about doing, when he was in trouble for something. Brad never blamed anybody else for his problems, never pointed a finger at anybody except himself. Their dad always talked about being accountable. Brad was the most accountable person Jack had ever known. So if he got grounded, or lost privileges of some kind, or had his phone taken away for a week or two, he'd always say the same thing to Jack: *I'm gonna wear it.*

Jack was gonna wear this, that was exactly what he was going to do.

What he wasn't doing, as it turned out, was walking home alone. Cassie Bennett took care of that, at his locker after their last class.

"Busing or riding a bike or walking?" she said.

"Walking."

"Good," she said. "I'm on your way. We can walk together."

Not even bothering to give Jack a vote.

"You live near me?" Jack said. "I didn't know that."

"A lot you don't know."

"You got me there," he said, "now that I've admitted I don't even know where your house is."

"No," she said. "I mean there's a lot you don't know, period. And not just because you're a guy."

He felt himself smiling again for the first time in a while.

"Got me there, too," he said.

They both had backpacks with them. Cassie wore shorts and a blue T-shirt with a little crocodile on the front and these canvas Converse sneakers almost the same color as her shirt, the kind with no laces. She had long hair Jack thought was more red than brown. She was shorter than he was, not by much. But it was like they always said in sports: Cassie Bennett played bigger.

He'd gone to a few of her softball games last year—that's how good she was, even boys went to watch her—and couldn't believe how good she really was. She looked like she belonged with the college girls you saw playing big-time softball on ESPN. When she'd go into her windmill windup and then underhand the ball to the plate, Cassie looked like she could strike out the world.

They walked away from school now, on Elm Street, on their

way to Main, where they'd take a right before they hit town. Then it was a long, straight shot to Jack's street, Running Brook Lane. Cassie said she was one block before that, on Head of the Pond.

"I can't believe we only live a block apart," Jack said.

"Callahan?" she said. "You gotta move past the whole geography thing."

Cassie was the one who finally brought up what had happened at lunch. She said she had always liked Gus, but that she hated bullies more, and he was acting like one in front of their whole class. And when she couldn't take it any longer, she'd stood up.

Jack said, "I hate when people are mean too."

"I'd never seen anybody ever call you out like that before," she said. She grinned. "You being the golden boy."

"Not feeling too golden today," he said. "Mostly I'm feeling like I let a whole bunch of people down."

"I didn't allow you to walk me home from school so I could listen to you feel sorry for yourself," she said.

"Is that how I sound?"

"Little bit."

But she was smiling when she said it.

They made the turn off Main, neither one of them walking very fast, neither one acting as if they were in any big hurry to get home.

Cassie said, "I'm just going to say this one time, just because I feel I know you well enough even though we've never spent much time together. Maybe that's because I think we have something in common, us being the two best baseball players in town."

She didn't act even a little embarrassed or self-conscious putting it out there that way, like what she'd just said was the most obvious thing in the world.

"It's about your brother," she said.

"Okay."

"I was at the funeral, not because I knew him, because I didn't. I'd just see him goofing around with his buddies in town sometimes. I was there because I felt so bad for you—and in a way, even for me, just trying to imagine what it would be like to lose my own big brother that way. I couldn't imagine what that would do to me in a million years."

"I didn't see you there."

"You weren't seeing anything that day," she said. "I was off to the side, watching you the whole time."

He turned to look at her and saw she was looking back at him, her face serious. And sad. Not the tough girl he'd seen in the cafeteria, the one who'd faced down Gus Morales, who was as tough as any guy Jack knew.

This was a different Cassie.

A new one.

A friend, maybe.

"My point being," she said, "that none of the people who think you should play, who act like you owe it to them to play, have any idea what it's like to be you. So don't listen to them. Listen to me: If you don't want to play, don't play, just like I told you at lunch. If this is some kind of delayed reaction or whatever to your brother, that's up to you to figure out, in your own way. Not them."

"Wow," he said in a low voice.

"Wow what?"

"Not only do you know me better than you think you do," Jack said, "I'm pretty sure you might know me better than I know myself."

She stopped in the middle of the sidewalk now. "You gotta be anywhere?"

"Not practice," he said. "But my mom's gonna be expecting me at a certain time. She knows pretty much to the minute how long it usually takes me to walk home."

Jack was about to stop himself there but didn't.

"She never used to worry about stuff like that," he said, "you know, before. But now she pretty much always wants to know where I am."

"Got it," Cassie said. "You got your phone? Call her and

tell her I kidnapped you as you were leaving school and you're gonna be late."

"Doesn't feel like I got kidnapped."

"Blah, blah, blah. Call her."

He did. Told her he was walking home with Cassie Bennett. His mom said, "The softball girl?" And Jack said, "One and the same."

"Have fun," his mom said. "See you in a bit."

He stuck his phone in the back pocket of his shorts and said, "So where we going?"

"You'll see."

The reason Jack's street was called Running Brook was that there was a brook running behind his house, one that fed into the Walton River, which ran all the way past the downtown area, behind the library and police station and firehouse.

Cassie led the way, down to the end of a street before hers called Journey's End, then down a narrow path through a small wooded area behind the last house on the street.

When they came out of the woods, Jack was standing in front of a pond that he'd never seen before.

"I didn't even know this was here!" he said.

Cassie made a motion in the air, like she was checking something off.

THE ONLY GAME   *45*

"One more thing you don't know," she said. "The list keeps getting longer and longer."

She smiled again. "The dock belongs to the Connors family," she said. "That was their house we just walked behind. You know Brooke Connors, from school? She's the catcher on our team."

Jack said that he did know Brooke. She could really hit. "I came to a few games last year," he said.

"I know."

"You do?"

"I saw you."

"You make it sound like you caught me watching you."

"Didn't I?"

"Whatever."

Now she said, "I come here to fish, by myself."

"You like to fish?"

"Not only like it, I can catch stuff like a champ. My dad taught me." She set her backpack down on the dock, and Jack did the same. Then Cassie walked back toward shore, reached down into the rocky stretch that passed for a beach, and grabbed a handful of smooth stones.

"But what I really like to do here is this," she said.

She walked to the end of the dock, faced the water, and took a deep breath that was more for show than anything else, Jack was sure of that. For his benefit.

Then she went into that flashy windmill softball windup of hers, Cassie the softball girl, and underhanded a stone that somehow skipped perfectly across the water.

Jack said, "Nobody can do that underhand."

"Said the boy pitcher to the girl pitcher," she said. "Well, I just did."

"If you can do it, I can do it."

Cassie motioned him to the end of the dock, reached into her pocket, came out with a stone, and handed it to him when he got to her.

"Should be no problem for you. This baby is much bigger than the one I skipped at least five times across the water."

"I can usually do this sidearm, no problem," Jack said, taking the stone from her.

"So can anybody."

He tried to imitate her motion, practicing it a few times, ignoring her giggles as he did. Then he took a deep breath of his own, went into his version of her windup, and watched as the stone landed barely ten yards in front of him and disappeared.

"I hate to say it," Cassie said, "but that thing dropped like, well, a rock."

Even Jack had to laugh.

She asked him if he had to be anywhere soon. He said no. She said, "C'mon," and led him through the woods as if she were some kind of guide, or had walked the path they were on a lot. Jack asked if he was allowed to know where they were going. She said no, but that he was going to be happy when they got to their destination.

"So there is a destination?" he said. "And we don't need to leave bread crumbs to find our way back?"

She said, "More walking, less talking."

Finally they came into a clearing, and Jack realized where they were. She had taken him all the way to the highest point in Walton, and maybe the prettiest. It was the area called Small Falls, with an old suspension bridge that connected one side of Walton to the other and gave you a spectacular view of the waterfalls and the rocks below them, water spilling out in the distance into the Walton River.

Jack remembered his dad taking him and Brad on walks there when he was little. The three of them would make their way across the bridge and over the falls, which didn't look so small to him when he was four years old. Jack had been afraid to look down, not only scared by the drop but by how loud the water sounded. Brad, of course, had talked about how he couldn't wait to go over those falls in a raft someday.

If he had ever done it, it was one secret that he'd kept even from Jack.

"Pretty great, huh?" Cassie said.

"I haven't been here in a long time," Jack said. "I forgot how awesome the view is."

"I come here all the time," she said. "I tell myself this is our town's version of Niagara Falls."

"That's what it looked like to me the first time my dad brought me here," Jack said.

"I was afraid when my dad brought me here the first time," Cassie said. "But I got through it."

"Shocker."

"It's the only thing you can do when stuff is jamming you up," she said. "You just gotta figure it out."

Jack wanted to tell her that sometimes that was easier said than done. But this wasn't a day to be jammed up about stuff. It was a day to just enjoy being with this girl. He only wanted to think about that.

"I don't bring just anybody here, just so you know," she said.

"So I'm not just anybody?"

She smiled and started to lead him across the bridge.

"Maybe you are," she said, "maybe you're not."

SIX

Jack and Cassie were sitting at the end of the dock a week later, having made their way back to the pond, legs dangling over the side, both of them having tested the water, still too cold to put their feet in, even on a warm afternoon that felt more like summer.

It was the third time they'd been here like this together, almost like their friendship was settling into a routine.

Jack knew that today's practice had already started for the

Rays at Highland Park. He mentioned it to Cassie, who said, "I know you think that's where you should be. But where you're at right now, with me, is where you belong."

"Was it Gus being mean, is that the only reason you stuck up for me the way you did? You were pretty mad."

"I don't even like it when people are mean to each other on TV or in the movies. I've never watched that old movie *Mean Girls*—the title alone bugs me."

"Were you worried that people would think you might be coming down too hard on Gus?"

"I was tough on him. There's a difference. And he had it coming."

Jack popped up now, picked up a stone out of the pile she'd made between them, and went back into her pitching motion.

This time the stone skipped.

Not five times.

But it didn't die a watery death.

When he sat back down, he saw her staring at him. "You hate looking bad, don't you?"

"I guess."

"Me too."

"But I don't see how I could look any worse right now, not being at practice. That's something I can't fix by skipping rocks across a pond, though I wish it were that easy."

"Sometimes you sound like you've got rocks in your head, Callahan. You gotta stop beating yourself up, or I may have to beat you up."

They sat without saying anything for a few minutes, the water in front of them still, the only sound around them from an occasional bird. You couldn't even hear cars from back here. He could see why Cassie liked it.

"I told you I don't know what it's like to be you, with your brother, I mean," she said finally. "But I know what it's like when people are pressuring you to do something you don't want to."

Jack waited.

Cassie said, "My parents are always trying to get me to do things they think are good for me."

"Like in sports?"

"Sometimes. They made me take tennis lessons, because my mom got it in her head that it was more of a girl sport than softball."

She put air quotes around "girl."

"And trust me, I could have been good at tennis—and I mean, like, great—but I wasn't going to open that door. Same as when they made me try figure skating. I just want to play softball."

"You're a ballplayer," he said, "just like me. Or like I used to be."

"Stop," she said. "But yeah, I'm a ballplayer."

"Only now you're telling me," Jack said, "that it's all right for me to not be a ballplayer."

"That's exactly what I'm doing. Go figure."

"But it makes sense to you?"

"What, you want to have a debate about it?"

"No, thank you."

She laughed. It was a good, loud laugh—nothing in her or about her was ever done quietly.

Or halfway, as far as Jack could tell.

"Just so we're clear," she said. "If anybody else gives you heat about not playing, you tell me and I'll take care of it. Or them."

"So you want me to tell them there's this girl I know who will beat them up?"

She said, "You think I couldn't?"

He put his hands up, as if in surrender.

"I can't believe we weren't friends before this," she said, "even if you are a guy."

"Agree."

"We really do have that in common, knowing what it's like to be the star of the team. Most kids don't. Or they think they want to be the star and don't know about all that comes with it. People watching every move you make."

"Like they are with me now."

"Yeah. Like that."

She turned and put out her hand, straight out, for Jack to shake. "We are officially forming a club," she said. "Two members only. The Jack and Cassie Club."

"I get top billing?"

"You've had a rough week," she said. "Just throwing you a bone."

Jack picked up one more stone out of the pile now, not planning to skip it this time. He pointed out a big old tree on the other side of the water and told Cassie it was his target. He cut loose with all the arm he had and hit it halfway up the trunk, the sound almost like the crack of a bat.

"They're right about you," she said. "You really do have some arm."

"Made for baseball."

Then he said, "Not gonna lie to you. Even if it only has been a few practices, I miss it already."

"Been thinking about that," she said. "Thinking about how much I'd be missing it if it were me."

Hands back on hips.

"Soooooo," she said. "If you decide you can't live without some kind of baseball in your life, you can come help coach my team. Mr. Connors was gonna be the assistant coach, but he told us yesterday he's gonna be traveling too much this month and next to give the team enough of his time."

"You're joking," he said. "Me? Coach a girls' softball team?"

She tilted her head to the side and said, "I'm going to forget I heard that attitude in your voice."

"I just meant you had to be joking about me being a coach," Jack said.

"We've only been friends for a week," she said. "But is there some vibe I gave off that makes you think I would ever joke about something as serious as baseball, Callahan?"

Then she said for him to think about it, they had to get going now, she didn't want his mom worrying.

"Look at how much has changed since that day when I took down Gus at lunch," she said. "Now you've got me worrying about you too."

They walked back through the woods, and then he walked her to her corner. She asked for his phone and put her number in, checking his contacts to see if there were any *A*s, then putting herself in as Bennett.

"I like to be first," she said.

"I picked up on that," Jack said.

Then she was running down her street. Jack watched her and wondered how a week that had started this bad for him could have turned out this good.

SEVEN

For a change, neither of his parents brought up baseball or the team or practice or anything at dinner. Jack got the feeling that they'd decided in advance to leave it alone for at least one night.

Or just give him some room.

That had been a big thing in their family after Brad died, how they all needed room to breathe.

"One foot in front of the other," his mom kept saying, until

it was a month since Brad's accident and then two, and then they were having their first Christmas without him and had now made it through most of a school year and were moving up on the first anniversary of the night it happened.

He'd heard his mom about a week ago on the phone, talking to a friend, heard that word—"anniversary"—and his mom then saying, "How can you have an anniversary for something you live with every single day?"

So they didn't talk about Brad tonight, or baseball, and Jack chose not to tell them about the way Gus was acting, what had happened with Gus at lunch, him and Gus and then Gus and Cassie.

They talked about Cassie instead, and his latest trip to the dock with her.

His mom said, "I didn't even know the two of you were friends."

"Neither did I," Jack said, "until lately."

He almost told them about Cassie's offer for him to help coach her team, still not sure if she was serious, even though she'd said she never, ever joked about baseball.

But he kept that to himself. Like Cassie'd said at the pond, he didn't want to open that door, at least not tonight. So he didn't put the subject of baseball back on the table.

"Homework?" his dad said when they were clearing the table.

"History test tomorrow," he said. "Woo-hoo."

"History was my favorite subject in school," his dad said.

"Good, you take the test," Jack said. "You probably still remember more about the Civil War than I'll remember first period tomorrow."

His dad said, "You'll be fine. Tests are just another way of keeping score. Seems to me you always do pretty well when somebody's keeping score."

Jack went upstairs to his room and studied for more than an hour. When he was confident he knew as much as he needed to know, he closed the book, happy that history was first period tomorrow. He liked to get tests and quizzes out of the way first thing.

He thought about seeing if there was a good game on television and decided against it. He didn't want to watch baseball tonight any more than he'd wanted to talk about it at dinner with his mom and dad.

He knew they wanted to, of course. Knew how much they wanted him to change his mind, wanted this season to be a happy-making time for all of them, the way it always had been.

But he couldn't.

That was the deal, no matter how much he missed baseball, before the Rays even played their first game.

"People say there's other games," Jack had said to Cassie at

Small Falls earlier that day. "But baseball's the only game."

"I know."

In his room now, he reached under his bed and pulled out his bat bag.

He unzipped it and took out the new Easton bat, the one he'd used last week to hit balls all over the field and finally hit one over the wall. Took his stance with it, but only after making sure that he'd locked his bedroom door, not wanting one of his parents, or both, to walk in and see him standing there in the middle of the room, like it was the top of the first of the first game of the season.

Top of the season.

Hands high, like his dad had taught him. Bat back, but not too far back. Wide stance but not too wide. The new grip on the bat felt perfect.

Jack started wondering, How many hits would there have been in this bat this season?

Then he put the bat down and sat on the bed with his Pedroia glove. A Wilson A2000. He had started last season using another Pedroia, an older model. But this one had been a Christmas present, and Jack had worked it in all winter, tying a ball into the pocket every night, putting it under his mattress, same as his dad had done with his new gloves when he was Jack's age.

Later on, watching TV at night, he'd sit there opening and

closing it, loosening it up. When it was the first official day of practice a year ago, he was ready to start using it in practice, alternating it with his gamer. Until it became his gamer.

It had been on his left hand in the championship game when he'd made one of the best stops he'd made in his life, a backhand play in the hole with the bases loaded, making the sidearm throw from his knees to get the runner at third and end the inning and keep the game tied at the time.

Absently now, sitting there, he began to open it and close it the way he used to.

In the quiet of his own room, he could hear himself saying what he'd said to Cassie on the dock.

Only game.

Then he put his bat away and put his glove away—his gamer—and zipped the bag back up and put it back where it had been under the bed. Like he was tucking baseball away.

Unlocked the door to his room.

He took out his phone and went to the top of the list. The *B*s.

Texted Cassie.

HEY.

She hit him right back.

HEY YOURSELF.

Jack typed.

GOT A QUESTION.

He thought he was fast. She was faster. Shocker.

U GOT QUESTIONS I GOT ANSWERS.

Jack paused now, staring at the phone in the palm of his left hand, where his Pedroia had just been. He shook his head before he hit her back, amazed at how much he'd already told this girl about himself, how fast he'd come to trust her. How much he wanted to be talking to her right now, more than anyone.

Even talking to her like this, in what his mom liked to call the "weird shorthand of the modern world."

Then he was typing again.

U SURE IT WILL GET EASIER???

Her answer:

Jack smiled. He should have known that Cassie Bennett would even text at the top of her voice.

SEE YOU AT SCHOOL.

Neither one of them had any idea that tomorrow at Walton Middle would be as eventful as last week had been.

More, in fact.

EIGHT

They had gym class right before lunch the next day, in the new gymnasium at Walton Middle that was almost as big and fancy as the one at Walton High School, one that Gus had always called Walton Square Garden. Theirs was the middle school version of that.

That was when things were a lot better and a lot different than they were right now between Jack and Gus. Now a long conversation between them, before a class or in the hall, went something like this:

"Hey."

"Hey."

Jack was sure that Gus wouldn't stay mad. He had never known Gus Morales to stay mad at anybody for very long, even guys on opposing teams. So it was impossible for Jack to believe Gus would continue to act this way with his best friend. How could he be this dug in?

But he was dug in for now, and everybody in their grade knew it.

"Don't let him get to you. That's what he wants," Cassie said between their history test and science. "He's acting like an idiot, and he wants you to act like an idiot."

Jack said, "He wants to be mad right now more than he wants the two of us to figure it out."

"Just keep putting one foot in front of the other," Cassie said.

Jack's head whipped around. "What did you just say?"

"It's something my mom says when she has a lot going on and starts to get stressed," Cassie said. "Why?"

"That's something my mom says."

Cassie leaned close to him and whispered in his ear. "Moms," she said. "It's like some weird cult."

It was time for gym class now, for the seventh-grade boys. Their teacher, Mr. Archey, was always looking for different ways to make the class fun. Maybe it was so they wouldn't notice how hard he was working them with his drills, or how tired they usually were when class was over.

But no matter how hard he did work them, their hour with him was the part of the school day Jack most looked forward to. It was all loud and competitive, even when they were just competing against themselves and the clock.

Most guys looked forward to it, but not all of them.

On their way from the boys' locker room, Teddy Madden said, "The Teddy Bear hour . . . about to begin!"

"Guys don't call you that all the time," Jack said.

"You just don't hear it the way I do," Teddy said. "Don't worry about it. I don't anymore."

"Just keep doing your best," Jack said. "Nobody can bust on you as long as you keep doing your best."

"Thanks, Coach," Teddy said.

"I bet you're a better athlete than you give yourself credit for," Jack said.

"You mean for somebody who's in worse shape than anybody in the whole school?"

Jack grinned. "You are not in worse shape than Mr. Cardwell."

Mr. Cardwell was the assistant principal and the size of a school bus. Gus once joked that when he got on a scale, the scale would say, "Hey, one at a time!"

"I meant students," Teddy said.

"Can I tell you something? You just need to get into better shape."

"Can I tell you something?" Teddy said. "The worst part of my day starts when I get into my gym clothes."

"C'mon, we just need to run that bad attitude right out of you."

"Are you kidding?" Teddy said. "I'm running right now, you just can't tell."

Jack had never realized how funny Teddy was. It felt like a welcome change today, going back and forth with him like this, just goofing around, especially now that Gus had put up a no-fun force field. Jack started to think that maybe he should be spending more time with Teddy Madden, who didn't seem to take himself too seriously, even if he refused to take sports seriously either.

Teddy was an interesting guy, not just some overweight clown. Jack wondered if he really could get healthier if he wasn't so down on himself about sports. He was overweight, no getting around that. But Jack could see that was at least partly because of the way he was built. He was never going to get skinny, even if he started working out now and didn't stop until they graduated from high school.

The real problem was that he was just so . . . soft. He wasn't clumsy, and Jack knew from watching him in gym that he wasn't as slow as someone his size should have been. But he didn't try and he didn't care, and when you're like that, you have no chance in sports, or anything else.

MIKE LUPICA

They had started class today shooting free throws at the side baskets. Mr. Archey put them in groups of five and used the big basketball scoreboard to time them. The guys on each team kept their own score before the buzzer sounded. Only the guys on the winning team didn't have to run laps today.

It was capture the flag after that. Everybody had a noisy good time with that, until Teddy, who was on Jack's team, ran into T.W. Stanley, who Jack thought might have stuck out his hip just enough, the way you did when you were trying to get away with a foul in basketball. It tripped Teddy up and he went down, sliding into the padded walls on that side of the court.

Teddy didn't look hurt. It would have been worse if he'd fallen on the other side of the court, where the bleachers folded back against the wall.

Jack ran over to help him up anyway.

"Make sure to see if the wall's okay, Teddy Bear," Gus called out from behind him.

The group of guys around him, including T.W., acted as if that was the funniest thing they'd ever heard.

"And now you know why I hate sports," Teddy said to Jack.

Jack looked down at him. He knew it wasn't the fall that was bothering Teddy. It was being made fun of. And right now it didn't matter that he'd told Jack he was used to it.

Jack pulled Teddy to his feet, thinking of an expression his dad liked to use. "It's just dumb guy stuff," he said.

Gus, though, wouldn't let up on Teddy, at least not yet.

"C'mon, Teddy Bear, you're fine," he said. "And by the way, it'll be time to eat soon!"

Hawk was with Gus and Scott Sutter and T.W. Stanley, laughing their heads off again.

Jack told himself they were all good guys. He didn't know for sure whether T.W. had intentionally tripped Teddy. Not so long ago he'd have said Gus was only chirping this way to be funny. But it wasn't funny today. It was mean.

Maybe Jack just hadn't been hearing it until now. Or maybe he was more aware of somebody being singled out this way because it had been happening to him the past few days.

Mr. Archey was over with them, to check out Teddy.

"You can't hurt me, Mr. A," Teddy said. "I've got all this padding."

Now Hawk wanted to get in on all the hilarity, saying, "Mr. Archey, that should be a penalty on the floor for tripping Teddy that way."

Gus added, "Maybe it would be safer for Teddy Bear to wait for the girls' class."

Jack turned around and said, "Shut up."

Teddy said, "Let it go."

"No," Jack said.

He walked across the gym to where Gus and Hawk and Scott and T.W. were standing.

"Somebody explain to me what's so funny about a guy falling down," Jack said.

"Chill out," Gus said. "You heard Teddy. Nobody means anything by it."

"You guys aren't funny."

"What, now you're Teddy's bodyguard?" Gus said. "Like Cassie is yours?"

"Yeah," Jack said, "maybe I am."

"Here's the deal, Jack," Gus said. "You don't get to be a team leader anymore. On account of you're not part of the team."

Jack said, "How long are you going to keep acting like this?"

Gus shrugged, then acted like he was talking to Hawk and Scott and T.W. and said, "How long does baseball season last?"

From behind them Mr. Archey said, "How about everybody chills right now and we get back to class?"

He gave them the option of finishing with dodgeball or kickball. He put it to a vote, the way he did sometimes. Dodgeball won. Mr. Archey agreed to play. He was really fast. He'd once been one of the best soccer players in the history of Walton. Everybody tried to nail him with the ball. Jack even succeeded a couple of times.

The game continued. Somehow, right before the end of class, Teddy Madden was the one holding the ball.

He looked to have Mr. Archey in his sights, right about mid-court. But then at the last second he wheeled and spotted Gus Morales on the far side of the court.

When Gus saw Teddy eyeballing him, he didn't even make an attempt to move. He just spread out his arms as if to say, *Come on*. Like there was no way that Teddy Bear Madden could hit him from that distance.

Jack watched Teddy's face now. He saw how determined he was in that moment, as if all of a sudden sports did matter to him. As if he did care. Then he stepped and threw a bullet that hit Gus in the stomach. The ball clearly knocked the air out of him and sat him down.

There were a lot of surprised seventh-grade boys in the gym at Walton Middle in that moment, including Jack.

None more surprised than Gus Morales, sucking wind.

"C'mon, Gus," Teddy called over to him. "Now it's time to go eat."

Teddy turned and walked toward the boys' locker room, looking a lot happier walking out of the gym than he had been walking into it.

And that was when Jack realized that maybe he wasn't as soft as he looked.

NINE

A couple of nights later Jack's dad came home from work early and asked if he wanted to go throw the ball around in the backyard before supper.

"A football?" Jack said, smiling at his dad.

"C'mon," his dad said. "Like we used to." Then, before Jack could say anything, his dad added, "Maybe a game of catch can at least feel like it used to around here."

"Okay," Jack said.

His dad went upstairs to change into a T-shirt and shorts and sneakers. He came back with his own glove, what he called an antique. It was an old Cal Ripken Jr. model. To Jack it was one of the coolest things in the world.

They began the way they always had, once Jack had started showing a talent for baseball. There were soft tosses at first. Then slowly they moved away from each other, until his dad was at the far end of the yard, by the small wooded area that led down to Running Brook.

Jack was standing right in front of the back patio to the house.

His dad said, "You better pay attention, because you miss one standing there and it might be a broken window."

It was the same thing he had been telling Jack since he was five years old.

"I don't miss," Jack said.

He didn't miss now, even as the throws from his dad began to come back with some zip on them. Jack felt some sting in the pocket of his Pedroia, but he didn't let on.

He thought, *Never let them see that you're hurting, in baseball or anywhere else.*

What did they always teach you?

Rub some dirt on it and walk it off.

Jack loved watching his dad play ball. Loved watching the way he threw. Loved the way even a simple game of catch could make him look happy. Sometimes he'd take one of Jack's throws, then make a sweep tag on an imaginary runner; or he'd tell Jack to throw him a hard ground ball, but not tell him whether it was going to be to his left or his right. Then his dad would be the one gliding to the ball, almost like he was floating across the grass. He'd glove the ball, plant his feet, and throw if it was on his backhand side. If the ball was to his left, he'd turn his body and flick the ball sidearm back to Jack.

His dad made one perfect throw after another. Jack hardly ever had to move. There was no danger of broken windows, none at all, even when Jack backed up near the house.

There wasn't much conversation. Both of them were into the catch. His dad did what little talking there was. Usually just a "Good" or "Attaboy." Or: "That's my boy."

After about half an hour, his dad said, "I give up."

"We just started."

His dad was walking toward the house now, saying, "If even this much baseball activity is tiring me out, I am officially out of shape."

"You looked good to me."

"You're a good boy. Now go get us a couple of Arnie Palmers."

It was their favorite drink, half iced tea, half lemonade. Jack went inside, got two tall glasses, poured two over ice, and brought them back out. They sat in silence watching the sun set over the water they knew was beyond the trees.

Through the open kitchen window they heard the news from the small television set on the counter, which usually meant his mom was starting to put together the salad that would go with their dinner.

"So," his dad said.

"So."

"How's it goin'?"

"You mean since the last time we had the talk we're about to have right now?"

He knew his dad wouldn't take offense, because he'd know that none was intended. Jack could talk to his dad in a way he couldn't talk with his mom, at least not now. It had gotten harder for them, him and his mom, since Brad died.

Jack was always afraid he was going to say the wrong thing and put that sad look back on her face.

"Just keeping the old lines of communication open," Tim Callahan said. "Like they tell you in the parents' manual."

"They've never been closed, Dad."

"I know."

"Doin' okay," Jack said.

"But you know why I keep asking, right? It was just that your mom and I were blindsided by this, even though you're not required to tell us everything that's going on."

"That's in the kids' manual," Jack said. "Not telling your parents everything."

"But the thing is," his dad said, "you've never kept the big stuff from us before. And this is big stuff."

Jack took a big swallow of his drink.

"I know baseball is big stuff to me the way it's always been big stuff to you," he said. "But it's like I said: I'm okay. And besides, it's only been, what, three weeks?"

"You had to take three days off last year when you jammed your thumb, and you told me it felt like three years."

"Baseball's not my whole life," Jack said, "even if I used to think it was. Before."

As soon as he heard the word—"before"—he wondered how many times that had been at the end of a sentence, or just a thought, since Brad had died.

Before and after.

"I get it, I do," his dad said. He turned his chair, and it made a loud scraping sound on the patio. He was facing Jack full-on now. "I get it and I get you. It's why I can't shake the notion that you're holding something back from us. From everybody."

Jack never lied to his dad. About big stuff or any stuff. But hadn't his dad just said that he wasn't required to tell everything that was going on inside his brain?

And he wasn't going to answer a question his dad hadn't even asked him.

"Dad," he said, "my heart's just not in it right now. It doesn't mean I love baseball any less. Or love you and Mom any less."

Now his dad was the one with the sad look on his face.

"We're trying so hard," he said, "your mom and me. Trying to be there for you. And at the same time trying not to try too hard to be there."

"You're not."

"You sure?"

"I'm sure."

"And you don't mind us talking"—his dad grinned—"no matter how often we've had the same talk?"

Jack shook his head.

"I just know one thing for sure by now," Jack said. "Talking doesn't change stuff."

"Doesn't mean it's a bad thing."

"Still doesn't change stuff."

"It's a variation of what my dad—your grandpa—used to say when I was your age. He'd tell me, 'Sorry doesn't fix the broken lamp.'"

Jack said, "Tell me about it."

His dad stood up and put his hand on Jack's shoulder, almost like he was using Jack to prop him up. Then he gave his shoulder a good squeeze.

"I understand if this is about Brad," his dad said, his voice quiet. "But even if it is, I just want to make sure you're doing what you're doing for the right reasons."

"I am."

That was the whole truth, nothing but, in Jack's mind. He'd thought things through the way his parents had taught him to. He was sure they were the right reasons.

He was sure he was right, even if he couldn't undo a wrong.

Even if he couldn't go back in time and fix the lamp.

TEN

It was the last Saturday before opening day for Walton Little League, baseball for the boys, softball for the girls. Cassie had finally worn Jack down enough to get him to come help with one of her practices.

Her team was the Orioles and was as much a favorite to win its league as the Rays had been to win the Atlantic, at least when they still had Jack.

The Orioles had Cassie, which meant they were the best.

"Your teammates aren't going to want to listen to me," Jack said.

"They will if I tell them to," Cassie said.

"Then you should be helping coach the team," Jack said.

"I'm not a coach," she said, making her voice deep, like she was trying to sound like an actress. "I'm a star."

"I forget sometimes," Jack said, and then Cassie was telling him to be at the school behind Walton Middle at ten o'clock and to bring his bat and glove.

"Yes, Coach," he said right before she hung up.

Cassie's dad was the coach of the Orioles. He'd played at Walton High School the same as Jack's dad had, just a couple of years behind him.

"Cassie tells me you've offered to help out," Chris Bennett said when Jack got to the field.

"It wasn't exactly like that, Mr. Bennett," Jack said. "I really didn't have much of a choice."

Cassie was standing between them, trying to look innocent.

Mr. Bennett nodded at his daughter and said, "Gee, that doesn't sound anything like her. Her mom and I have worked so hard trying to get her to come out of her shell."

"I am doing you both a favor," she said. "You can't work with everybody at once, Dad. And Jack needs to be near the game, whether he'll admit that or not."

"There you go, Jack," Mr. Bennett said. "Neither one of

us seems to realize how lucky we are to have her."

"Hey!" Cassie said.

Mr. Bennett asked Jack if he could handle infield practice, while the coach worked the outfielders on catching fly balls, learning to hit the cutoff man, and knowing where to throw the ball when there were runners on the bases.

"There's this idea in Little League that your best fielders are in the infield," Mr. Bennett said. "I keep telling the girls that a missed ball in the infield usually means somebody getting one extra base. You miss one in the outfield, it's *lots* of extra bases."

"You go ahead, Dad," Cassie said. "I'll help Jack out with any stuff he's forgotten."

"You wish," Jack said.

Cassie played shortstop when she wasn't pitching, same as Jack. Angela Morales, Gus's sister, played third, Katie Cummings was at first, Gracie Zaro was at second, and Brooke Connors was behind the plate.

Before they started infield work, Jack pulled Cassie aside and asked if Angela was cool with him being here. There hadn't been any further trouble between Jack and Gus over the past couple of weeks, but only because Gus was avoiding Jack as much as possible.

Cassie said, "She thinks her twin brother is acting like an idiot too."

MIKE LUPICA

"He's not an idiot," Jack said. "He's just hurt."

"So you're not mad at him, even the way he's been treating you?" Cassie said. "Or not treating you?"

Jack shook his head. "Gus wants to play in the big leagues someday. That's his dream. And part of it is that when he gets there, they go back and show him playing in the Little League World Series. So in his mind, it's like I'm messing with his dreams."

When he stopped talking, he saw Cassie staring at him, her face serious for a change.

"You know who isn't an idiot?" she said. "You."

Then she ran out to shortstop.

Jack hadn't been kidding with Mr. Bennett. He knew he was here today because Cassie really hadn't given him much of a choice. But after a few minutes, he found himself getting into it. Being back on a ball field, with a bat in his hands and a beautiful Saturday morning spread out in front of him the way it used to be, felt good.

Not only that, if he was here to coach, he was going to be the best coach he could be.

When Cassie bobbled a ball after moving to her left, Jack called out to her, "You should have been in front of that ball."

"Oh," she called back from shortstop, hands on her hips. "Is that the way this is going to go, Callahan?"

Jack felt himself smiling.

"That's *Coach* Callahan," he said.

A few minutes later a ball went under Gracie Zaro's glove at second base. Jack dropped his bat, jogged out to where she was standing, and showed her how to put her arm and her glove straight down, the glove right in the dirt. That way it was easier to have it already down there when the ball got to her.

He reminded her to keep her head down. She needed to look the ball into her glove every single time one was hit to her.

"It's not just outfielders who need two eyes and two hands on the ball," he said.

He kept things moving, hard grounders and slow rollers, even calling out, "Let's get two!" once in a while.

"You really think we're going to get double plays?" Cassie said.

"I guarantee you and Gracie will turn one in a big spot this season," Jack said.

"In your dreams," she said.

But then she was the one gliding to her left, making a perfect underhand toss to Gracie, who made the transition from glove to ball and made a sweet throw to Katie Cummings at first.

They were good, Jack thought, not just Cassie. Not that he would tell any of them that, because he didn't want them to think he was surprised because they were girls.

He wasn't just impressed by how well they were fielding, but by how much they all seemed to enjoy being out here. The same as he enjoyed being out here.

Jack knew that coaching wasn't the same as playing, wasn't the same and wasn't as good. Nothing was better than being a real player. But he had to admit, this felt pretty great.

He told himself it didn't count as playing, it was more about being a friend to Cassie, doing this because a friend had asked him to. He wasn't breaking any rules he'd set for himself by doing that.

After they finished with fielding, in both the outfield and infield, Mr. Bennett told everybody to get a quick drink and then it would be time for batting practice.

"You think I didn't notice that the grounders you hit me were twice as hard as the ones you hit everybody else?" Cassie said when they got to the bench.

"But there was a reason for that," he said.

"Like what?"

Now he was the one using a deep voice and trying to sound like an actor reciting his lines.

"You're a star," he said.

She laughed, and so did he. Jack wasn't just happy to be on this field, although he knew that was a part of it. He was happy to be on this field with her. And he knew that he'd be spending a big chunk of the afternoon with her in town, once Cassie did some clothes shopping with her mom right after practice. They were planning to have pizza at Fierro's, and then maybe go to see a movie.

"It's a movie about a high school football player," Cassie had informed Jack. "So it won't be torture for you even though there are no car chases or exploding buildings."

When all the players on the Orioles had hit, Mr. Bennett asked Jack if he wanted to take a few cuts against Cassie. He did it in front of the whole team. Just the suggestion that he might stand in there against Cassie brought a lot of whoops and hollers from the other girls.

"No, thank you," Jack said. "I don't want to affect her confidence—we all know how she struggles with that, Mr. Bennett."

"What's the matter?" Cassie said to him. "You afraid to get shown up by a girl?"

"Your dad's a lawyer, Jack," Mr. Bennett said. "I think he'd advise you not to answer that."

Jack looked around, pretending to be confused, saying, "You think there's someone here who could get me out?" He finally looked at Cassie and said, "Oh, you were referring to yourself?"

"Grab a bat, funny man," she said.

The last time Jack had taken his batting stance was back in his room. The last time before today that he'd even unzipped his bat bag.

Now he went over to where he'd laid his bat down in front of the bench. He picked it up and walked toward home plate as Mr. Bennett sent the Orioles out onto the field. Cassie was already on the mound. Brooke Connors was behind the plate in her catcher's gear. Angela Morales moved from third to short, and Molly Rather went to third in her place.

"Hey, outfielders," Mr. Bennett called out, "if Jack hits one your way, remember what we worked on this morning."

"The outfielders aren't going to get any work," Cassie said.

Jack actually felt his heart pumping, bat in his hand, pitcher on the mound.

He told himself to make sure he looked like he was having as much fun with this as Cassie and her teammates were.

But he was not going to get shown up by a girl.

Even this girl.

No one was enjoying the moment more than Cassie Bennett.

She took her time, milking the moment for all it was worth. She turned her back to Jack, checking her fielders, even moving her leftfielder, Erin Merrill, closer to the leftfield line.

Finally she turned back around, smiling like she was sure that whatever happened next was going to be the highlight of her day.

Cassie Bennett was that sure of herself.

She went into her windmill motion and promptly threw her first fastball right past him, Jack swinging over it. By a lot.

"Strike one," she said.

"You need three to strike me out," he said.

"That's the plan," she said.

Jack watched her, thinking that she felt the way he always did when he was the one on the mound with the ball in his hand, looking in at the batter and thinking, *You cannot beat me.*

He reminded himself that this was a softball she was throwing. Every time he and Gus and the guys would goof around playing softball, the ball would look as big as a melon to him. But as big as it looked, you had to concentrate just as much as you did hitting a regular baseball. Even though the ball wasn't coming at you as hard, and you had more time to wait, you couldn't get overanxious and lunge at the ball prematurely, because the result would almost always be a pop-up.

But when you did start your swing, you had to make sure you hit through the ball with a short, level swing, because if you swung too hard with an uppercut swing in softball, the result was usually a weak pop-up.

Cassie went back into her motion, the second pitch higher than the first, high enough to have been called a ball if this were a game and there were an ump calling balls and strikes. Jack knew, as a pitcher, that this was the one you wanted the hitter to swing at. The ball was nearly up in his eyes, which meant it was usually a pop-up waiting to happen, if the guy got his bat on the ball at all.

Jack went for it, taking a huge rip, just getting a piece of the ball, fouling it straight back over Brooke Connors's head and into the screen.

"Strike two," Cassie said, and her teammates cheered louder now than they had for strike one.

Jack stepped out of the box, bent down, picked up some dirt in his right hand, and straightened back up the way he would in a real game when he was trying to collect himself. He rested the bat on his belt buckle, rubbed the dirt on both hands, gripped the bat again. He'd always loved the way the handle felt with a little dirt on it.

As much as Cassie and her teammates were loving this, Jack knew it was time to get serious.

She is not striking me out.

Even if he wasn't technically a ballplayer right now, he still remembered how it felt to be one.

He knew that if this were a real game and he were pitching, he would probably try to get the batter to chase a bad pitch on an 0–2 count. If he knew that, Cassie did too, because she wasn't just a good pitcher, she was a great one.

But she was showing off now, for him and for her friends. He just knew she wasn't going to waste a pitch, she was going to come right at him, try to get strike three right now.

It was like the TV announcers said after a three-pitch at bat for some hitter: Good morning, good afternoon, good night.

Cassie rubbed up the ball, more of the show. That's when Jack saw Teddy Madden, whose house was right across the street from the school, leaning over the fence on the third-base side of the field.

Teddy put a hand in front of his own eyes, pretending he couldn't bear to watch what was about to happen.

Jack took his stance. *Wait*, he told himself. It was one of the first things his dad had ever told him about good hitting. *Stay back and wait.*

Cassie went into her motion one more time, arm whipping forward as if she wanted this to be the hardest pitch she'd ever thrown in her life.

But Jack was on this one, taking a short stride, turning into the ball and his swing with perfect timing, and remembering as he did what it felt like to catch a ball on the sweet spot of a bat.

He watched the softball heading toward dead center now, thinking it had enough to get over the wall, not knowing for sure because it wasn't a hardball.

Cassie knew.

She was right there in Jack's line of sight. He could see her and the ball, see that Cassie wasn't even turning around to watch. Because she knew.

As the ball sailed over the centerfield wall, clearing it by a lot, Jack couldn't resist.

"Do I need to run around the bases to make the home run official?" he said.

Cassie shrugged, not giving in to the end.

"Knock yourself out," she said.

But he didn't run. He just walked back to the bench, put his bat back in his bag, and closed it up, trying not to show her up, or show how great he felt.

This was going to be the only home run he hit all season, and he had to admit: He'd take it.

ELEVEN

Cassie had gone off to shop with her mom, saying she would meet Jack for pizza in an hour. She was going to cut shopping short, because she was getting hungry already for at least two slices at Fierro's. The rest of the Orioles players had been picked up. Jack and Teddy were sitting together on the home team's bench, first-base side.

"I really did think she was gonna strike you out for a second," Teddy said.

"She would never have let me live it down."

Teddy said, "Knowing Cassie, it would have been her favorite Facebook post of all time."

Jack had thought about walking home but knew that by the time he got there, it would practically be time to turn around and go meet Cassie in town. So he and Teddy stuck around, talking about the practice and his home run. Jack admitted to Teddy how good it had felt.

Because, man, it had felt that good.

Maybe that was the real reason he wasn't ready to leave the field yet.

"Hey," he said to Teddy, "I've got some time before I have to go meet Cassie for lunch. You want to play some catch?"

"You want an honest answer? No."

"It'll be fun. Do you have a glove?"

Teddy patted his pockets, the way you do when you're looking for something. "Not with me," he said.

"Go get it. You live a minute away."

"I don't want to play catch."

"But I do," Jack said.

"I thought you quit baseball."

"I'm not talking about a comeback," Jack said. "Just a game of catch."

Teddy sighed loudly, stood up, and said, "I knew I should

have kept walking past school. Or started running."

"Run now, and get your glove."

Teddy was back five minutes later with a couple of bottles of Gatorade—"I can tell I'm gonna need some refreshment"—and a catcher's mitt that looked almost brand-new.

"You just get that?" Jack said.

"Got it two years ago. For my one and only year of Little League. I'm pretty sure that if I'd left the tag on, my mom could still get her money back."

Jack took out his Pedroia, grabbed one of the old baseballs he always carried around in the bat bag, and said to Teddy, "Well, let's finally break that baby in."

A lot had changed for Jack, but not this, not today:

He didn't want to leave the field.

It turned out that despite all his complaining, Teddy could throw a baseball better than he could throw a dodgeball in gym class. A lot better.

He still didn't look like much of an athlete. Still looked too soft, even though Jack would never say it to him like that.

But the guy could definitely throw.

"You've got a good arm," Jack said.

"Awesome," Teddy said. "Can we stop now?"

"No, we have to work on your catching," Jack said. "You just need to focus."

"I don't want to focus," Teddy said. "I want to get back to doing what I've always done best in sports."

"What's that?"

"Sitting down."

"You have the worst attitude, you know that, right?"

"It's one of my best things," Teddy said, grinning. "I am *great* at having a bad attitude."

"We need to change that."

He hadn't told Teddy to grab his glove with any kind of plan in mind. But one was starting to form.

"Just because you like coaching girls now doesn't mean you have to start coaching me. Not gonna happen."

"See, there's that bad attitude again."

"Which I'm good with!"

"No, you're not," Jack said. "You don't want the other guys making fun of you, and neither do I."

"It doesn't bother me all that much, even with what happened at gym the other day."

"It bothered you enough to nail Gus with the ball."

"Gotta admit, that was sweet," Teddy said. "But I'm not lying when I tell you that stuff doesn't bother me as much as you think it does."

"But it bothers me now that we're friends," Jack said. "It makes me feel bad. And it will make me feel worse if I don't do something about it when I know I can."

"By making me into a ballplayer?"

"Maybe just getting you into shape."

"Oh, that's your job now?"

"Our job," Jack said.

"And this is important to you why?"

Jack said, "It just is."

He pointed toward home plate and said, "So let's go."

"You mean we're not done?"

"Nope."

They walked across the infield, Jack telling Teddy to get behind home plate like a real catcher would.

"You want me to catch you?"

"I promise I'll go easy on you."

"What does that mean, you're going to throw lefthanded?"

Jack told him to get down into his crouch. Then he walked to the mound, aware in that moment that it was the first time he'd stood on a mound since last season.

"Ready?" he said to Teddy as he toed the rubber.

"Heck no!"

But to Jack's surprise, Teddy actually looked a little bit like a catcher once he took his position behind the plate, even though he told Jack that once he was in his crouch he might not be able to get out of it.

After about fifteen minutes Jack said, "Okay, explain to me why you stopped playing Little League when you did."

"I couldn't run and I couldn't hit. I figured those two things were kind of crucial to being a good baseball player."

"Who told you that you were too slow, your coach?"

Jack's dad always said that way too many coaches worried way too much about what kids couldn't do in sports as opposed to what they could. Jack wondered if that's what had happened to Teddy.

"It wasn't anybody's fault. I just didn't love it," Teddy said, almost not even noticing as he made a decent backhand stop and sidearmed the ball back to Jack from his knees. "And when I told my mom I didn't love it and probably wasn't going to get to play very much, she let me quit and take guitar lessons."

Teddy's parents, Jack knew, were divorced, Teddy having told him the other day that his dad was living all the way across the country in Oregon and hardly saw him at all.

"So basically you took the easy way out," Jack said.

"Look at you!" Teddy said. "Figuring out another one of my best talents!"

Jack turned and walked to second base, telling Teddy he wanted to see if he could make the throw all catchers had to make, from Little League to the big leagues, if they wanted to throw out guys trying to steal.

Teddy could make the throw.

He bounced the first couple and occasionally would sail one over Jack's head—Jack knew you had to have some arm to be able to do that—but most of the throws were around the bag.

"You should be playing baseball," Jack said.

"Wait, isn't that what everybody's saying about you?"

Jack was walking back toward the plate. "This isn't about me, it's about you. Like I said, all you need to do is get into better shape."

"This is my shape."

"Let me help you."

He was surprised in that moment how much he meant what he'd just said. How much he wanted to help Teddy Madden, no matter how much Teddy kept finding funny ways to say he didn't think he could be helped.

Jack wasn't sure he understood why it was this important. Or why Teddy's attitude was starting to frustrate him the way it was.

"I'm a little confused," Teddy said. "You don't want to play, but I'm supposed to want to?"

"There's nothing worse than not trying," Jack said.

His voice was louder than he'd expected.

"I already tried once," Teddy said. "And could you chill a little?"

Jack felt himself getting hot all of a sudden. "You didn't try hard enough," he said. "Obviously."

"You don't know that," Teddy said. "You barely knew me at all until a couple of days ago."

"I'm just asking you to let me try to get you into better shape," Jack said.

"You make me sound like some kind of school project."

"It's not like that."

"But it sounds like that, because you need something to do. You know what I really want to do right now? Get a drink."

They walked over and sat down in the grass next to the home-team bench, then opened the Gatorade bottles Teddy had left there.

"Jack, you gotta let this go," Teddy said. "You're starting to sound like you want to save me from a fate worse than death or something if I don't get in better shape. It's not like I'm out playing in traffic or something and you have to save me from a speeding car."

In that moment everything that had been happening to Jack the past few weeks, with his parents and with Gus, just exploded out of nowhere. It was as if everything he had been holding in and holding back came out of him in a rush. Nothing he could do to stop it. He didn't even try.

"Sometimes people don't see when they need saving!" Jack said, shouting now at Teddy, feeling himself start to cry as he said, "My brother didn't."

TWELVE

Jack was trying to breathe, get some air into him, get control of himself, so he didn't start blubbering in front of Teddy Madden.

He wanted this to be over.

More than that, he wanted to take back what he'd just said. But he couldn't.

He saw Teddy staring at him, eyes wide, like he was afraid to say anything. Or even move.

When he did speak, he said to Jack in a quiet voice, "Dude, why don't you try to drink some Gatorade?"

Jack did that now, coughing a little as he tried to drink too much, still not able to get enough air. Still feeling like he might cry if he wasn't careful.

"Sorry," he said finally.

"No need to apologize."

They sat there in silence until Teddy said, "What just happened?"

"Got a little carried away, is all," Jack said.

Teddy said, "What did you mean just now? About your brother needing to be saved?"

"I didn't mean anything."

"I'm not slow about everything, Jack," Teddy said. "Didn't you just say we were friends?"

Jack nodded.

"Well, now let me help you," Teddy said. "Be your friend. What are you telling me about your brother?"

"I don't want to talk about it."

"Well, guess what, you just did," Teddy said. "I'm just thinking you didn't finish what you need to say."

Jack didn't say anything. He just picked up the ball lying next to him in the grass, stood up, and walked a few feet away from Teddy, back out to the mound. Then he faced home plate and threw the ball as hard as he could and maybe as hard as he'd ever thrown a ball. Like he wanted to burn a hole in the screen.

Like he was letting more than the ball go.

He came back and sat down next to Teddy. He wasn't sure why, but he trusted him. It was time to tell somebody his secret.

"I could have saved him," Jack said. "My brother."

He paused before adding, "It was my fault that he died."

THIRTEEN

They had basically moved the baseball field at Walton Middle the year before so they could build new tennis courts, but the one thing they'd managed to keep was an old-fashioned dugout on the third-base side of the field.

Jack pointed to it now and said, "Can we go sit over there?"

It wasn't like he wanted to walk down the old cement steps and hide in the dugout. It was too late to hide, too much already out in the open now. Or about to be.

Somehow it just seemed more private over there.

"Whatever you want," Teddy said.

The guy who always had something to say looked like he was afraid to say anything right now.

They left their baseball stuff in the grass and walked across the infield, Teddy carrying both bottles of Gatorade. When they got into the shade of the dugout, they sat at the far end.

It was Jack who spoke first.

"I'm trusting you," he said.

"I know."

"I haven't told this to anybody," Jack said. "I'm not even sure why I'm doing it now."

Teddy said, "It just sounded to me like one of those things you couldn't hold in anymore." He gave Jack a quick, nervous smile and said, "But what do I know? I'm pretty much an idiot."

"No, you're not," Jack said. "Or I wouldn't still be here."

He stopped now and looked down at his baseball shoes.

Then Teddy was the one taking a big deep breath, saying, "You said you could have saved your brother. But that's crazy, right? Everybody knows it was an accident."

"It's like they say. Brad was the accident, just waiting to happen."

He started to feel the tears coming again but squeezed his eyes shut, telling himself that he wasn't going to let it happen, that he'd come as close as he was going to come. Truth was, he'd thought before today that he was cried out about his big brother.

"I didn't know him," Teddy said. "But everybody in town knew what a wild man he was."

"Nobody knew better than me," Jack said. "But he never listened to me about stuff, when it wasn't stuff about baseball."

"Hey, you were his little brother."

"But that's not really what I was talking about."

"I don't get what you meant when you said he needed help," Teddy said, "or saving."

"From himself," Jack said. "Every time he'd get away with something wild, he'd already be thinking about the next thing."

Teddy said, "I remember seeing him one time, riding his skateboard, holding on to a school bus. I mean, how nuts is that? Waving at everybody as he went by. He had this look on his face like what he was doing was the greatest thing in the world."

"He finally did it one too many times, and the police ended up bringing him home," Jack said. "He told my mom and dad he'd learned his lesson, until the next time he hauled off and did it. When he let go of the bus, he went flying into a parked car and cut his forehead and ended up needing six stitches. But he told Mom and Dad it had happened at the skateboard park. Made me swear not to tell the truth."

"And you didn't."

"I thought I was being the brother he wanted me to be," Jack said. "He used to tell me all the time he knew his secrets were safe with me, that he trusted me more than anybody."

Teddy handed him the Gatorade bottle, and he drank what was left in there. When he finished, he patted his back pocket for his phone before he realized he'd left it on the other side of the field. He wasn't sure what time it was, but he didn't think he and Teddy had been talking long enough that he was going to be late meeting Cassie.

Teddy shrugged. "I only want to know if you want to tell me."

"Trying to," Jack said. He took a shaky, deep breath and told Teddy about the night Brad had come home and charged into Jack's room, all excited. He'd closed the door behind him, keeping his voice down as he told Jack that his friend Nick, who was already sixteen, had let him drive his dad's car on one of the country roads outside town.

"I couldn't believe what I was hearing," Jack said. "Brad was still, like, three months away from turning sixteen himself. He didn't even have a learner's permit. He just laughed at me and said that the only way to learn was by doing."

About three nights before he died, Brad came back from dirt-biking and showed Jack this huge scrape on his chest. "He said that he'd been going too fast racing the other guys. He'd gotten thrown and said it was like he'd gone sliding headfirst into third base."

Teddy smiled a little at the phrase.

"That time he didn't even have to make up a lie," Jack said. "He just made sure my parents didn't see him without a T-shirt on for a few days. So he didn't have to lie and I didn't have to feel like I was telling one either."

"But it was like you said, he trusted you."

"He trusted me so much that I'm here and he's gone," Jack said. "Because I went along and never said anything."

Now the tears started to come, and he couldn't stop them. He just tried to wipe them away with the back of his hand.

"All I had to do that night was say something to my parents," Jack said. "I knew where he was going. I knew what he was doing. I knew it was dangerous. He'd just fallen off that stupid bike three nights before."

"You can't blame yourself for that."

"Yes, I can."

Teddy said, "But you said it yourself, he was always looking to take the next chance."

"But I could have stopped him this time."

"And you never said anything to your mom and dad?"

Jack shook his head. "They would have told me what you

just did, that I shouldn't blame myself, that it wasn't my fault that my brother got taken away from me. But they would have been wrong."

In a quiet voice Teddy said, "You're wrong, Jack."

Jack shook his head and said, "And no way they would have understood why I had to find a way to pay for that."

A voice from behind them said, "That's why you did it, isn't it?"

It was Cassie.

Jack and Teddy both looked up and saw her standing above them at the corner of the dugout. She was staring at Jack.

"That's why you quit baseball."

Jack was full-on crying now. He just nodded.

FOURTEEN

The boys got the Little League fields at Highland Park on Saturday mornings, and the girls played their softball games in the afternoon.

This was the second weekend of the season, and Cassie's team was already 3–0. They were on the same schedule as the boys, one game under the lights during the week, another game on Saturdays, all the way until the play-offs at the end of the school year.

Jack was still an assistant coach with the Orioles, and he was liking the job more and more. He actually felt as if he was helping some of the girls on the team get better. Mr. Bennett kept telling him that if he saw something one of the girls—including Cassie—was doing wrong, to show them how they could do it better, whatever it was, hitting or catching or throwing or running the bases.

"I can see now why people always talked about you having a gift for baseball," Mr. Bennett had said to Jack one night at practice. "Right now you're doing a thing called paying it forward."

And Jack had kept working with Teddy the past couple of weeks, coaching him, too. He wondered if Teddy agreed because he was afraid to turn him down. He wondered if Teddy was worried about upsetting him. Whatever his reason, Teddy stopped complaining and threw himself into the practices.

Jack and Teddy hadn't talked about Brad since that day at the field. And Jack made Teddy and Cassie promise they wouldn't tell anybody.

Teddy agreed and didn't bring it up at all. But of course it was different with Cassie. She was Cassie, and she was different from anybody else Jack knew. It was no shocker that she thought there were different rules for her.

"Just because you and Teddy don't talk about this doesn't

mean we're not," she said when they were walking to Highland Park one morning. "Guys are dumb that way. Totally. But girls talk about stuff."

"Okay," Jack said. "But now that you know everything, I don't know what else there is to say."

"Oh, there's still a lot to say."

"I know you want me to tell my parents," Jack said. "But that's not happening, no matter how much pressure you put on me."

"Having an opinion is not pressure."

"With you it is."

Cassie said, "You do remember that I'm the one who told you not to play if you didn't want to play, right? But that doesn't mean I'm not allowed to think your reason for not playing is messed up."

"I get that, okay? I think even people in outer space get that by now."

"I just think they could talk some sense into you even if I can't," Cassie said.

"My parents or people in outer space?"

"Both!"

"Just let me coach," Jack said. "I'm having fun being a coach. Isn't that enough for you?"

"I just don't think it's enough for you," Cassie said.

Jack looked over and saw her smiling. Her Orioles cap was

turned backward on her head, even though she never did that when she was on the field. She was old-school about baseball the way Jack was, another reason why he liked her as much as he did.

"You want me to drop this now?" she said.

"Whatever gave you that idea?"

They walked the rest of the way to the field in silence, even though he knew she wanted to say more, because she always had more to say, about everything. And there were things he wanted to say to her sometimes—like now—about how he wondered all the time whether being around the game, even if it was a girls' softball team, made him miss playing even more.

Because no matter how much he liked helping these girls, and helping Teddy, Cassie was right. Coaching baseball didn't come close to playing baseball. He saw this interview one time with John Elway, who he knew had been one of the great quarterbacks of all time with the Broncos, talking about what it was like to run the Broncos team now. Elway was the guy who'd signed Peyton Manning. He said how helpless he felt watching somebody else try to make the throws and plays he used to make to win the game.

Maybe the thing that made Jack feel most helpless now was that the Rays, which he felt was his old team, had gotten off to such a lousy start without him. They'd lost two of their first three games.

Gus would always come and watch his sister play. Today he was sitting on the Orioles' bench, still in his Rays uniform, when Jack and Cassie arrived at the back field. The front of Gus's uniform was full of dirt, and his head was down.

Jack walked over to his best friend—his former best friend—and asked the question, already knowing what the answer was going to be.

"How'd you guys do today?"

"Lost," Gus said. "To the White Sox. We were ahead, but then Andre came in to pitch the last two innings and walked the whole world. We went from winning 6–4 to losing 9–6."

"That stinks."

"Tell me," Gus said. "We should be unbeaten, and we're 1–3 instead."

"You guys will figure it out," Jack said. "The team's too good for you not to figure it out. I read that the Yankees—the real ones—started out 1–3 in 1998 and ended up winning a hundred fourteen games and then the World Series."

Gus said, "I'm not worried about that World Series, just the one in Williamsport."

He started to say something else but didn't, just got up and walked out to where Angela Morales was warming up with Katie Cummings down the rightfield line. Jack watched him go and thought, *At least we're not fighting anymore.*

They were talking. He felt good about that, even though he felt horrible about the Rays' record, knowing that Gus and everybody else on the team must still feel as if he were letting them all down.

Cassie came and sat down where Gus had been. "How's he doing?"

"They lost again, that's how he's doing."

"Yeah, I heard," she said. "Did he try to blame it on you?"

"No, but he probably wanted to. He probably still wants to be yelling at me, but maybe he finally figured out it just ends up making both of us feel lousy."

She said, "You guys will be friends again."

Jack said, "Not if he feels like I'm the one who cost him a chance to make it to the Little League World Series."

"What about your chance?" Cassie said.

"It means more to him."

"You keep telling yourself that," she said, and then asked him to warm her up.

Mr. Bennett coached third base for the Orioles, while Jack had become the regular first-base coach. Mr. Bennett had even given him his own orange Orioles cap, with the bird on the front.

There wasn't really a lot to do coaching first. You just reminded base runners to go halfway on a ball hit in the air to the outfield and told them to run hard with two outs as soon as the batter put the ball in play. Stuff like that. Cassie's first time up she ripped a ball down the leftfield line. When she was halfway to first, Jack was already waving his arm, telling her to keep going to second. He could see she was going to have an easy double.

A moment like that made him feel like he was part of the action, or as close to the action as he was going to get unless he caught a foul ball hit in his direction.

The Orioles won, 7–1, the other team getting their only run long after Cassie had stopped pitching. She had gone the first three innings today, striking out six batters. Jack watched her after every one, saw how cool she was about it. He hoped he looked that cool when he was pitching—never showing up the batter, never pumping a fist, just waiting for the infielders to throw the ball around.

Jack would never tell her this, just because her head was so big already he was afraid it might explode if he paid her one more compliment about her baseball ability. But he loved watching her pitch.

Truth was, he just loved watching her play.

More than anybody, more than Gus or any guy he knew, Cassie reminded him how happy playing ball could make you feel, especially if you could play the way she could.

She went to shortstop after finishing her three innings on the mound. She made the last out of the game by picking up a slow roller a few feet to the right of the pitcher's mound, fielding the ball cleanly, and snapping off a sidearm throw to Katie at first. Only then did she allow herself a fist pump.

While the Orioles players celebrated their victory between the mound and first base, Jack looked into the bleachers to where Gus had been sitting. He thought he might ask Gus to hang out, the way they used to hang out on Saturday afternoons.

But Gus was gone.

Jack was in town with Cassie and Teddy after Cassie's game—he always thought of them as hers, never his own—and the three of them were sharing a pizza when he remembered he hadn't turned his phone on after the game ended.

When he turned it back on, he knew he'd messed up. He hadn't even told his mom he was going into town for lunch.

There were three missed calls that said HOME.

The same number of text messages, asking him where he was.

"Oh man," he said, staring at the phone in his hand. "I am going to be in huge trouble."

Teddy, mouth full of pizza, said, "You don't get into trouble, you're Jack Callahan. I'm the one who gets into trouble."

Jack told them what had happened, and Cassie said, "Go outside and call her right now."

He walked out of the restaurant and speed-dialed his mom.

When she answered, he said, "Mom, I know what you're going to say. I am so sorry."

"Where are you?"

He told her.

"You didn't tell me you were going for pizza."

"I know," he said.

"I don't know why I kept leaving messages. I could tell the phone was off."

All he could do was apologize to her again.

"We had a deal," she said.

"I know."

"I need to know where you are," she said.

"I know," he said again.

"It's not so much to ask, is it?"

"Mom, I'll say it again," he said. "I'm sorry."

She asked when he'd be home and he told her in a couple of hours, that he was going back to school to throw a ball around with Cassie and Teddy. Cassie loved showing off her hardball skills every chance she got.

"If you're going to be later than that—"

"Call," he said.

He walked back into Fierro's, thinking that his mom didn't know how sorry he really was, no matter how many times he'd said it.

Today had been a good day up until that point, watching Cassie pitch, feeling like things were getting at least a little better between him and Gus.

Normal, almost.

Then Jack remembered, all over again, what normal really was now.

It was this.

Normal was his mom worrying that something might happen to him.

FIFTEEN

He let Cassie pitch to Teddy, with a regular baseball, over-hand. Of course she looked good enough to be pitching in the boys' league, which she was threatening to do next season. Jack watched her and thought that maybe if she'd been the one pitching in relief for the Rays today, they would have won their game instead of lost it.

Cassie would be a strike thrower in any league.

But as well as she could throw, Teddy got some hits off her, solid ones. Jack chased the balls down in leftfield, occasionally getting a long run when Teddy, a right-hand hitter, would hit a ball to the opposite field.

The running didn't bother him. It felt good to be out in the field, his Pedroia mitt on his left hand, in the sun on a nice day with the two people he most wanted to be with these days.

And it felt good watching Teddy start to get confidence, even if he was only doing it for an audience of two.

Later, when Jack and Cassie were walking home, the two of them having long-tossed in the outfield after Teddy said he needed to go take a rest, Cassie asked if Jack wanted to go fishing off the dock.

But he said he'd better go straight home. He felt like he owed his mom a little of what she called her "Jack time."

"You worry more about other people than anybody I know," Cassie said.

"Gus would probably argue with you on that one."

"But see, he'd be wrong!" Cassie said. "Because you're still worrying about him."

"He's my friend," Jack said. "You've got to be a good friend even when they're not around. My dad calls it being a friend behind somebody's back."

"You're even better at being a friend than you are at baseball."

They were at the corner to Cassie's street by then.

"Don't you mean than *you* are at baseball?"

"Excellent point," she said, and patted him on the back, saying she'd text him later and then running down the street, like she was racing against herself.

His mom was in the kitchen when he got home. He knew it as soon as he walked through the front door: The smell of her chocolate chip cookies filled the whole house and maybe the whole neighborhood if he'd kept the door open any longer.

He walked into the kitchen saying, "Can I skip dinner and go straight to dessert?"

He could see one huge plate of cookies cooling on the kitchen counter and knew that meant another batch was in the oven. Once his mom started baking cookies, she couldn't stop.

"Dinner's in less than an hour," she said. "You may have one."

"One?" he said. "You're asking me to have just one of your chocolate chip cookies. Your warm, just-out-of-the-oven, chips-making-a-mess-on-your-hands chocolate chip cookies? That's way too much punishment for me forgetting to call."

"You're under the impression that you have a strong negotiating position?"

"Two cookies," he said.

"Two and then a shower," she said.

"Deal."

She smiled. Jack loved seeing his mom smile, especially

because she didn't do it often enough these days.

He got himself a glass of milk to go with the warm cookies. The two of them sat at the table, his mom having told him that his dad was still on the golf course.

"Might be the best chocolate chip cookie ever made," he said.

"Don't talk with your mouth full. And you always say that."

"But is it working for me?"

"Always," she said, and smiled again.

It was one of those moments when he wanted to make sure he didn't say anything to make the look on her face go away as quickly as it had arrived. He didn't want it replaced by that sad look that would come into her eyes out of nowhere. He made himself busy—happily—eating her cookies.

She asked how his day had been, and he told her about how well Cassie had pitched, how amazing she was.

"Amazing as a softball player?" Gail Callahan said. "Or just amazing, period?"

"Mom," he said.

"Yup, that's me, your mom, asking you about a girl."

"I know what you're asking me."

"Seemed like a pretty simple question."

"She's amazing as a player, that's what I meant."

She made a motion like she was wiping sweat off her forehead. "Whew!" she said. "Glad we cleared that up."

She was still working on the cup of tea she had been drink-ing when Jack came in. She seemed in no hurry for him to go up and shower. He told her about how much better Teddy was getting, how a couple of weeks ago he wouldn't have had a chance to get a hit off Cassie.

"Maybe the talent was there all along," his mom said, "and it took you to get it out of him."

"I'm a solid coach, but I'm not that good."

"If it's anything to do with baseball," she said, "sorry, but you are that good."

The two cookies were long gone. She said, "Go ahead, you can have one more." She trusted he'd still have an appetite after an afternoon of baseball. She sipped some tea. The only sound in the kitchen was the ticking of the big wall clock near the tiny television she kept on the counter so she could watch the news while she fixed dinner.

"It must be hard sometimes," she said finally, "playing ball but not really playing."

"Kind of," he said. "But that's just part of the deal."

He saw a slight raising of one eyebrow. "What deal is that?"

"Just a figure of speech, Mom," he said. "All I'm saying is that it's just part of it. I knew I wasn't going to be able to avoid baseball totally when I quit the team. You know what I'm say-ing, right?"

She sipped more tea. "Not really, no. It's not like baseball has sought you out. Seems to me like it's the other way around."

She smiled again.

"It just worked out that way."

"I guess," she said. "But you go to two of Cassie's games a week as a coach, you help coach two practices, you've become Teddy's personal instructor. Just seems to me you're on the field as much as ever."

"But you get that it's not the same as playing, right?"

"Which you won't allow yourself to do." Still in a soft voice.

"No," he said, knowing as soon as he did that he'd answered too quickly. "It's not about not allowing. It's about not wanting to."

"Right."

"So you get that," he said. "Right?"

"Even though playing has always made you so happy," she said. "Now you can't allow that."

"That's you talking, Mom, not me."

"Just talking to my boy is all," she said. She put her hand over her teacup and leaned forward. Smiled again. "Not trying to pressure you, honey. We never put any pressure on you to play sports."

"I feel enough of that from the guys on the Rays," he said, "even if they're not talking about it at school anymore."

"My whole thing is for you to be happy," she said. "And like I said, I know how happy baseball always made you."

"It's different now, is all. Between me and baseball."

Jack heard a car outside and hoped it was his dad, hoped that he'd heard the front door open, so he could close down this conversation. But it must have been one of the neighbors' cars.

"I guess what your dad and I don't understand," she said, "is how right after you pushed baseball away, you let it start pulling you back, even though no one made you."

"Maybe I can't explain it, but it's working for me."

"Explain the reason you can't play," she said, "is that what you mean?"

"The reason I don't want to play," Jack said.

"Right," she said again.

He felt as if he were spinning his wheels now. Or being spun around. All he'd wanted was some cookies.

"Mom, you gotta stop."

"What, talking to you? I've told you your whole life that we were going to talk to each other, whether you wanted to or not. That's our deal. At least until you made this decision on your own."

"I feel like we've talked this to death."

"Around it. Never got right to it. Why you felt like you just had to do this."

"I didn't have to do anything!" Jack said.

Compared to the way his mom had been speaking to him—that low, soft voice—he knew it sounded like he'd shouted at her all of a sudden.

He sighed. "It was just something I felt like I had to do."

"You just told me, and loudly, that you didn't have to do anything."

He didn't just feel as if he were being spun around now. He felt himself getting dizzy.

"You're twisting my words," he said.

She reached across the table and put her hand over his.

"Honey, you're the one who seems all twisted up."

"I give up," he said as he pushed his chair back and stood up. "Thanks for the cookies, Mom."

He rinsed his plate and glass, put them in the dishwasher, and walked out of the room and up the stairs, trying to understand why he felt the way he used to when he walked back to the bench after striking out.

SIXTEEN

He called Cassie as soon as he closed the door to his room.

"My mom acts like she knows something," he said.

"About what?"

"About the real reason I quit."

He told her what had just happened in the kitchen, making sure to keep his voice down. Then he said, "I gotta ask you something: Did you say something to her?"

There was a pause at the other end of the line, a long one, too long.

"I'm going to act like I didn't hear that," she said.

"Sorry," he said. "But the whole conversation was just . . . weird? I felt like I was in a courtroom or something, not my kitchen."

"Because of the questions she was asking you?"

"Not just that, the way she was asking them. Like she knew more than she was telling. I swear, Cass, the way she was looking at me was like she was looking all the way inside me. Does that make sense?"

"Parents see stuff," she said, "even when we think they're missing everything."

There was another pause, and she said, "You told me to swear not to tell. I don't go back on that. And neither would Teddy, but with him it's because he's afraid of you. As cool as he likes to act, he still can't believe you want to hang out with him."

"Stop."

"I'm just sayin'."

"I'm not saying that my mom knows everything," Jack said. "But I had to get out of there, because I started to feel like if I stayed, I'd spill my guts to her the way I did to you and Teddy."

"Why don't you?"

"Because it wouldn't change anything," he said. "All she'd do is what you do, and tell me I'm wrong to *think* the way I do."

"Mostly because you are wrong."

"No," Jack said. "You are, unless you think things wouldn't have worked out differently if I'd just said something."

Now Cassie was the one shouting. "Say something now! You've been beating yourself up long enough. Can't you see that?"

"You're the one who told me not to play if I didn't want to."

"That was before I knew the real reason why," Cassie said. "Will you please listen to me for one minute?"

"I am listening. I always listen to you," he said, adding, "Not that I have much of a choice."

"I'm being serious."

"So am I."

Cassie said, "I am gonna tell you something, and if when I'm done you want to hang up on me, go ahead."

"Okay."

"So here goes," she said. "If something hadn't happened to your brother that night, it was going to happen eventually. And, Jack, guess what? Maybe he was lucky it hadn't happened already."

"You don't know that."

"And you don't know if stopping him from getting on that stupid bike that night would've stopped him from going the next night! Or the night after that! I know I really only know your brother through you. But I feel like I know him now."

Jack waited.

"You still there?" she said.

"Still here."

"C'mon, Jack. What's one of the first things we hear from our parents? Don't play with fire. Brad's deal was that he loved playing with fire the way you love baseball."

"Loved baseball."

"Don't be an idiot," she said. "You think I'm the one missing things? You love it more than you ever did."

"So now I'm an idiot?"

"Yeah, about this you are. You know how you've made this big thing out of helping Teddy? You gotta let your parents help you."

He heard the front door slam downstairs, heard his father announcing that he was home, and this was it, he meant it this time, he was quitting golf, the sport hated him.

Cassie said, "Can I say one more thing?"

"Sure."

"Every time we talk about Brad, you tell me how much you loved him and how much he loved you, right?"

"Yeah."

"You think he'd want you to do this?"

It stopped Jack, because he'd never thought about it that way. And he told Cassie so.

"You know the answer," she said. "He wouldn't have blamed you, and he wouldn't want you to punish yourself this way."

"You don't know that, either."

"Nope, I don't, you got me there. But it's what I think. And I wouldn't be a real friend if I didn't tell you what I think about the big stuff."

There was a picture of Brad, his favorite, above his desk. It was one his dad had blown up for him, and it showed the first time his brother had ever gotten up on a surfboard and stayed on it, one summer when they'd rented a house on the ocean for a week.

"You've kept enough of his secrets," Cassie said. "Good night, Jack."

And she hung up.

SEVENTEEN

They didn't talk about baseball at dinner. Jack thought that maybe his mom had said something to his dad about not bringing it up. So the conversation was mostly about what his dad said had been a disastrous day of golf.

"That's it, I'm giving up golf," he said. "And I really mean it this time."

Gail Callahan said, "And we really believe you!"

"Mom," Jack said, "I think Dad means it way way more than he did all the other times he quit and said he really meant it."

"Go ahead, both of you, have your fun," Jack's dad said. "Maybe you'll believe me when I pick up another hobby."

"Maybe one you could complain about less?" Gail Callahan said.

They all had ice cream for dessert, with a plate of his mom's cookies on the side, and then Jack's parents said they had a movie they were going to watch on the big screen in the den. Jack told them he might watch a movie of his own upstairs.

"Not R-rated," his mom said.

"It's *Happy Gilmore*," Jack said.

"Again?" she said.

Jack said, "I like to watch it so I can see golf making at least one person happy," and shrugged at his dad, who said, "Very funny, smart guy."

It was weird. It was as if the talk he'd had with his mom over cookies had never happened. Or maybe she felt she'd said everything she needed to say on this day.

He was in his room a half hour later, still trying to decide between *Happy Gilmore* and a ball game, when he found himself walking down the hall to Brad's room.

It was still his brother's room, and it wasn't at the same time.

The poster from *The Hangover* had been taken down along with the rest of his movie posters. There were still family pictures on his desk, including Jack's favorite, from last year, of Jack in his baseball uniform, holding up his MVP trophy, Brad standing next to him in cargo shorts and a *Sons of Anarchy* T-shirt, his arm draped over Jack's shoulders, both of them smiling.

Most of his other stuff from the room, laptop and CDs and books and magazines and clothes—not that his brother ever had a lot of what he called big-boy clothes, he preferred shorts and T-shirts and jeans and sandals—had been packed away in boxes and stored in the basement a couple of months after the accident.

When Jack asked his parents why they were taking most of Brad's things out of the room, his dad had said, "It will always be his room. But we don't want it to be a shrine, either."

Jack didn't go into the room very often. He hadn't gone in there for a long time after Brad died. He just couldn't deal with the fact that when he opened the door Brad wouldn't be there, wet towels on the floor along with dirty clothes. Brad wouldn't be stretched out on his bed, eyes closed, hands pressing his headphones to his ears, listening to music, rap music, usually.

Jack walked in there now and sat down at what had been his brother's desk, replaying in his head the conversation he'd had with Cassie.

Would Brad have wanted him to quit?

Or blame himself for what happened that night?

Would his big brother have wanted Jack to wear that?

He sat at the desk for a long time until his mom walked in so quietly she made him jump.

"You scared me," he said.

"You weren't in your room," she said. "I wondered if you might have gone for a walk or something without telling us."

"I wouldn't do that at night."

"What are you doing in here?" she said. "You told me you don't like being in here."

"Thinking."

"Always a good thing."

She sat down at the end of the bed and patted it as a way of telling him to come sit next to her. When he did, she put her arm around him.

They sat there, neither one of them saying anything, in this room that always seemed more empty and quiet than any other place in the house. After a few minutes his mom said, "I want you to tell me what you haven't told me."

And he did.

Finally he did.

Jack told her all of it, not rushing, telling it at his own pace, trying not to leave anything out.

When he finished, he put his head onto her shoulder and cried. His mom pulled him closer and, as she did, yelled down for his dad to come upstairs.

When he came into the room, Jack's mom said, "Tell your father what you just told me."

It was easier this time, no tears, his dad sitting on the other side of him.

His dad turned Jack so they were facing each other. Jack saw that his dad's eyes were red.

"You have carried this around all this time?" Tim Callahan said, sounding like he might cry.

Jack nodded.

"I am going to say this one time, son, and then I am never going to say it again," his dad said. "What happened wasn't your fault, isn't your fault. If it was anybody, it was me. And your mom. You think we haven't asked ourselves and each other a thousand times why we didn't make him stop the things he was doing?"

"But I was the one who should have tried to stop him that night," Jack said. "I was the one who knew he was going."

"You would have betrayed his trust," his dad said. "He trusted you to the end."

"He was who he was, your brother," his mom said. "You are who you are. He wouldn't have loved you as completely as he did if he couldn't have trusted you with his secrets. Because those secrets, honey? They were part of who he was too."

"Cassie said I've kept secrets long enough," Jack said. "Mine and Brad's."

"She's right," his dad said. "It's time to let them go."

They sat there on the end of the bed, Brad's room quiet again except for their breathing, until his mom got up and told Jack she had something to show him.

EIGHTEEN

It was a small box, badly wrapped.

Jack knew that Brad had done the wrapping; it had always been a family joke. He was the guy who loved rap music but was such a bad wrapper of presents. But Brad still insisted on doing his own wrapping himself.

It was why when they looked under the tree on Christmas morning, they could spot Brad's gifts immediately.

The way Jack could now.

"I found this when I was going through his things," his mom said. "I didn't know what it was or who it was for, so I opened it. When I found out it was for you, I taped the paper back together."

She smiled at him. But now she was the one starting to cry. It made Jack feel as if they were all watching the same sad movie together.

"There's a note inside," she said. "Also for you. You'll see when you read the note. It was supposed to be your birthday present last fall. But then it seemed . . . I couldn't bring myself . . ." She shook her head. "I just thought it would all still be too sad for you."

She started crying again. Jack's dad said, "Then we decided we would save it and give it to you on opening day of the baseball season." He lifted his shoulders and dropped them. "But then there was no opening day, and so we didn't know what to do with it."

"Your brother always said that opening day of the season was more like Christmas for you than Christmas," his mom said.

Jack said, "He said to me one time it was even more than that, like Christmas and New Year's wrapped up into one holiday. He told me that as far as I was concerned, that ball they drop in New York on New Year's Eve ought to be a baseball."

His mom said, "I've been waiting for just the right time. Your dad and I both. And after everything you've told us tonight and everything we've talked about, now seemed right."

The box was in Jack's lap. And if it had been Christmas, he would have torn right into it. Not now. He carefully pulled off the wrapping, bit by bit, like it was part of the present.

When he opened the box, he saw the baseball, sitting in a plastic stand. When Jack picked up the ball, he saw this:

To Jack: Never give up. Your friend, Dustin Pedroia.

"Is this . . . ?"

"Real?" his dad said. "It is."

Jack rolled the ball around in his hand, feeling the seams. Then he held it up in front of him again, still not believing his eyes, and looked at Pedroia's signature.

"How?" he said.

"We've been trying to figure that out since your mother found it," his dad said. "But you know what your brother was like."

"One more secret," Jack said.

"You know what he was like," his dad said. "Go big or go home. How many times did we hear that? Somehow he got to Pedroia. Or he knew somebody who could get to Pedroia and get this done."

"He never said anything about it?"

His dad shook his head. "He must have gotten it sometime before . . . sometime last summer. He was obviously going to surprise us all with it."

His mom said, "Now read the note."

It was in a small envelope, underneath where the stand for the ball had been. *Little Bro* was scrawled in Brad's terrible, little-boy handwriting on the outside.

But the note had been printed out.

Hey, he'd written. *I'm writing this late at night, which I read in a book once is the time when guys tell each other the truth. So this is the truth, little bro, even though it sounds a little lame now that I'm gonna write it down. It'll probably never see the light of day when I give you the ball.*

But just in case I change my mind, I wanted you to know something that an older brother never tells his younger brother, which is this:

You're my hero.

Jack saw the paper shaking a little in his hands, but he kept reading.

I wanted to get you a baseball present that would mean something to you. Maybe because I know I've never been as good at anything as you are at baseball. Or loved anything other than you and Mom and Dad the way you love baseball.

(Man, this is starting to feel longer than a paper for school!)

You know what I always tell you, how slow I think baseball is. Hated playing it. Still hate watching it on TV. But here's one more secret, me to you:

I love watching you play. Always have, always will. I know that someday I'll be watching you play at Fenway Park or Yankee Stadium. Maybe by then I'll have found something to be as good at as you are pitching or hitting or running the bases.

But I'll still be watching you. Proudly, little bro. Who knows? Maybe this ball will be some kind of good luck charm for you next season, on your way to the LL World Series. Or maybe you don't need luck.

Anyway, if you ever see this, happy birthday.

I love you.

Brad.

He didn't cry when he finished. He felt himself smiling, the letter in his right hand now, the ball in his left.

All along, he'd wanted his brother back, even if it was just for one more day.

And now he was.

NINETEEN

After church the next morning Jack's dad said, "You're going to need to talk to Coach Leonard, you know."

"I need to talk to Gus first," Jack said.

He had thought about calling him last night before bed, after he'd talked to Cassie and told her what he'd done, told her about the ball, Brad's letter, everything. But by then all he wanted to do was sleep.

And he decided against calling now. Jack thought it had

been so long since he'd picked up the phone and just called Gus, or texted him, or Facebooked him that it would feel weird.

What was he going to say in a message?

COULDN'T WAIT TO TELL U. CHANGED MIND, WANT TO BE YOUR TEAMMATE AGAIN AFTER ALL, NO WORRIES!

No, this was a conversation he needed to have with Gus Morales in person.

He knew Gus and Angela and their parents usually went to church at nine. So they would be home by now, Mrs. Morales cooking up her huge lunch for them, always big enough to feed a small army.

Jack changed out of his own church clothes and put on jeans and a T-shirt and sneakers. His mom asked if he wanted her to drive him over. Jack said no. He'd do that on his own too.

"I got myself into this, I'll get myself out of it," Jack said. "I never look for help when I'm the one who loaded the bases."

He went out and opened the garage door and wheeled out his bike. It wasn't a fancy speed bike; the farthest he ever took it was to Gus's house, about a mile and a half away. So he didn't need what his dad called bells and whistles. He didn't need hand brakes or any of the other things you saw on faster, sleeker bikes. His bike, which Gus loved making fun of, was so old-fashioned it even had a basket attached to the handlebars.

"Go ahead and crush me if you want," Jack had told Gus one time. "I'm even old-school with bikes."

And Gus had said, "Yeah, I think guys used to try to get away from dinosaurs on bikes like yours."

Jack was all the way to the street when he stopped. He put down the kickstand, left the bike near the mailbox, ran back into the house and up to his room, went under his bed, and took his glove and ball out of his bat bag.

Then he went into his closet, reached up on the top shelf, and pulled down the Rays cap that Coach Leonard said he could keep when his mom called about taking back his uniform.

Gus lived in the opposite direction from Cassie's house, heading out of Walton, almost to the Lewisboro line. Before Jack left, he'd given one more quick thought about calling, just to make sure he wasn't wasting a long ride over there. But he wanted this to be a surprise. He hoped Gus would be okay with him wanting to come back to the Rays, and he hoped Gus wasn't still blaming him for the team's 1–3 start, and the hole they'd put themselves in.

Maybe Gus thought it was too big a hole for them to climb out of. The Rays were sitting in next-to-last place, and three other teams in the league had started out at 4–0. But Jack wanted to play, if his friends would let him.

It was a perfect day, Jack thought, for baseball or anything else. There were no clouds in the sky, hardly any breeze. On the way over he thought about how many times in his life he'd taken this same ride to Gus's house after church on a Sunday morning. Somehow, though, this felt like the first time.

"A new beginning." That was what his mom had talked about the night before.

She made it clear that just because Jack had told them his own secret and just because he wanted to start playing baseball again, that didn't change what had happened with Brad. Nothing ever could. Jack playing baseball was never about that. But this was another way, a good way, for all of them to move forward.

It was different with Gus. At least with him, Jack could make things the way they used to be.

As he came around the corner of Smith Ridge Lane, he saw Mr. Morales's blue van parked in the driveway. It meant they were home.

Mrs. Morales answered the door. She was wearing her apron, wiping her hands on it. The smell of the food she was cooking—probably her usual feast of rice and beans and pasta and chicken or steak or both—made Jack feel as if he'd come back to what had always been his other home.

"Jack Callahan!" Maria Morales said, gathering him into her arms. "What a wonderful surprise!"

"Nice to see you, Mrs. Morales," he said, wondering if she could even hear him with his face pressed into her shoulder.

"We have missed you so much," she said. "Does Gustavo know you were coming?"

"He doesn't."

She stepped back now from Jack and yelled up the front stairs to Gus that there was somebody to see him. Then she pulled Jack into the house as if she was afraid he might jump on his bike and ride away.

"Gustavo Morales!" she yelled again. "Can you not hear your mother calling to you?"

Gus came walking out of his room. "I was on the phone, Mama."

When he saw Jack, he stopped.

Jack could see the surprise on Gus's face. But all he said was, "Hey," like Jack being there was no big deal.

"Hey," Jack said.

"I'm sorry," Maria Morales said, "is this talking, or texting?"

She motioned for her son to get down here.

He was wearing one of his favorite T-shirts. BIG PAPI was written over an image of David Ortiz, one of the great

Dominican players of all time. That alone would have been enough for Gus to love him as a player. But Jack knew it was more than that. David Ortiz was one of the great World Series players of all time, from any country.

To someone who dreamed as hard as Gus did of making the Little League World Series, what Ortiz had done in his three trips to the Series for the Red Sox was pure magic.

Gus came down the steps and stood in front of Jack. Both of them sensed how awkward they felt in the front hall. They didn't bump fists. They didn't give each other a quick high five. They didn't lean in with their shoulders.

They just stood there.

Finally Jack said, "I need to talk to you about something."

"So talk," Gus said.

"Gustavo Alberto Morales!" his mom said.

"What?"

"I am going to leave you alone to talk to your friend Jack now and also pray to the Lord that you remember your manners while you do."

She walked back toward the kitchen. When she was out of earshot, Gus said, "So what did you want to talk about that we couldn't talk about on the phone?"

"Everything," Jack said.

• • •

They went and sat where they had sat a lot in their lives, after Sunday lunch and after school and after games, on the front porch of the Morales house, five steps up from the walk to the door. They had always called it "the front stoop," just because Gus's dad always had.

"It was a stoop in Santo Domingo," he'd explained to Jack once, "and it's still a stoop in America."

Jack talked for a long time. Gus listened. He didn't say a word the whole time, until he finally said to Jack, "You finished?"

"Pretty much."

"I'm your best friend," Gus said. "Why didn't you tell me?"

He wasn't talking to Jack about baseball, or what him coming back would mean to the team. He wanted to talk about their friendship. He made it sound as if this were another way that Jack had let him down, in a bigger way than just leaving the team.

"I just tried to explain," Jack said. "I didn't tell anybody."

"But when you did, you told Cassie and Teddy before you told me."

Gus was staring past Jack's bike, out at the street.

"I didn't plan that," Jack said.

Gus shook his head. "We always told each other everything," he said. "We told each other we'd always tell each other everything."

"I messed up," Jack said. "I messed up not telling my parents where Brad was going, and I've been messing up ever since."

"You just sat there and let me call you out the way I did in the cafeteria," Gus said. "I never would've done that if I'd known."

"I know," Jack said.

They sat there in silence. This wasn't going the way Jack had thought it would on his way over. More than anything, he'd thought Gus would be happy that he wanted to play for the Rays again. He'd just assumed Gus would focus on what this meant for the team and for him, because of how important baseball was in his life.

Jack should have known him better. Should have known that friendship and loyalty mattered even more to him.

"It's like you didn't trust me enough," Gus said.

"It wasn't about that!" Jack said. "It's what I'm trying to tell you now. I thought I'd worked it out right in my head, but I worked it out all wrong. Because you were my best friend, you would have tried as hard as my parents to talk me out of doing what I was doing."

"You think with me it would've been all about the team."

"If I ever did think that," Jack said, "I know better now."

It was almost as if Gus wasn't listening now, as if it was almost more important to him to get things off his chest.

"I would have wanted what was best for you whether you decided to play ball or not."

"That's something else I know now."

"But you always should have known."

"You're right," Jack said. He smiled, trying to somehow break through the wall he still felt was between them. "This may be the most you've ever been right at one time."

He looked at Gus and said, "Right?"

Gus wasn't smiling back. "So what do we do now?"

"First thing, I have to talk to Coach, see if he even wants me back on the team."

"Okay, now you do sound like an idiot," Gus said.

"I never even asked you if he'd filled my spot."

"He tried, with Justin Horton," Gus said. "But you know how good Justin is at lacrosse, and his coach told him he didn't want him to play both, even though the town allows it. So Coach just decided we'd go with what we have. He said it would mean more playing time for everybody."

Jack said, "I thought I'd call him after I talked to you, maybe go over from here and talk to him if he's home."

"I'll go with you," Gus said.

"You don't have to do that."

"I didn't say that I thought I had to, I said I would," Gus said. "Idiot."

"Okay."

Gus pointed at Jack's bike and said, "You brought your glove."

"If you didn't tell me to get lost, I thought maybe we could throw the ball around or something. Unless you wanted to throw one at my head after you heard me out."

Gus gave him a shove now. A playful one.

"Meet me in the backyard. I'll go get mine," Gus said. "Do I even need to ask if there's a ball in the pocket of that glove?"

"You do not."

When Gus came back out of the house, they went to the far end of the Moraleses' yard, not quite as big as Jack's, but close enough, enough space to put some distance between them, and some air under their throws.

Before long they were laughing the way they always had back here, trying to knock each other's gloves off the closer they got to each other.

It was like they were back to speaking their own language, through the game they both loved the way they did. They didn't need words. Jack and Gus started to tell each other through baseball that things were going to be all right between them.

Mrs. Morales asked if he could stay for lunch. Jack called his mom, who said, "Of course." After lunch—Mrs. Morales's cooking was even better than Jack remembered—he and Gus rode their bikes to Coach Leonard's house. Mrs. Morales had called ahead. They sat with Coach Leonard in his living room, and then Coach was the one hearing out Jack's story. Coach was the one hearing how much Jack wanted to come back and play.

When he finally ran out of words—feeling like he'd run out of gas—Coach just said, "See you at practice tomorrow night."

"Thank you."

Coach smiled. "No," he said. "Thank you. How's the arm, by the way?"

"Better than ever," Gus said, answering for him the way he used to, and they all laughed.

It was when he got home later that his parents said they had one last thing to show him. "Haven't I had enough surprises?" Jack said.

Then she walked him up the stairs and into his room.

There on his bed, perfectly laid out, was his Rays uniform.

Pale blue. Number 15. Pedroia's number, of course.

"You didn't take it back when you said you did."

"Nope."

"It was here all along?" Jack said.

"It's like you always tell me," his mom said. "Just in case a game broke out."

TWENTY

Y ou're late," Coach Leonard said when Jack showed up for practice Monday night.

"But, Coach," Jack said. "It's only five thirty. Practice doesn't start until six."

He looked around. Only about half the Rays were there. Even Gus hadn't arrived at Highland Park yet.

Coach Leonard grinned at the guys who were there and said, "I meant late for the season."

Jack had been worrying about how the rest of the Rays would react to him, but it turned out he shouldn't have. They made it easy for him right away, even before the whole team was on the field.

"No kidding," Gregg Leonard, Coach's son, said. "About time you showed up."

Scott Sutter, their catcher, said, "If you'd waited any longer, I was afraid we were going to fall behind girls' teams in the standings. Now go get a ball. We need to start warming up that arm right now."

Jack looked at Coach. "Okay to start throwing?"

Coach made a show of checking out his watch. "You've been here five whole minutes," he said. "I was afraid you'd never ask."

When Gus showed up, he walked over to where Jack and Scott were throwing near first base. Ignoring Jack, he called out, "Hey, who's the new guy?"

"Some scrub," T.W. Stanley said from the infield grass, where he was warming up with Gregg.

Gus stood there and watched Jack throw for a couple of minutes and finally said, "Does this guy actually intend to pitch with that arm? I've seen more arm strength from guys brushing their teeth."

"Let's see how you feel the first time I brush you back in batting practice," Jack said.

It went like that for the first half hour of practice. Jack's teammates busted his chops every chance they got. Jack would occasionally come back at them with chirp of his own. Mostly he took it. Never in his life had he been happier to be the object of trash talk.

It was as if this was a different kind of baseball language, his teammates' way of letting him know how good they felt about him being back.

Just not as good as he felt.

Nobody asked why he'd quit the team in the first place. Maybe Coach had told them not to ask. Or maybe Gus had told the rest of them to leave it alone. It would mean Gus had Jack's back the way he used to.

When the last of the Rays, Brett Hawkins, showed up about ten minutes before six o'clock, Jack had gotten alone with Coach Leonard and asked if he should say something to the team.

Coach said, "Everything that was needed to be said has been. What matters is that you are here."

Jack didn't tell him, but it was a tremendous relief. On the way home from Coach's house the day before, he'd told himself that he was never going to tell the story about Brad, and why he'd done what he'd done, ever again. If any of his teammates did ask, he was simply going to tell them, "My head wasn't in it. Now it is." Hopefully he would be able to leave it at that.

Coach was right. He was here, that was what mattered. His head was back in it now. His heart was in it too.

All in.

Before batting practice started, he asked Coach where he wanted him to hit.

"Third," John Leonard said. "Right before Gus. Like always."

Gus heard that.

"And you get you're not facing a girl now, right?"

"You heard about that?"

"My sister said it was the only time in her life she was ever rooting for you to strike out."

"Believe me, I was afraid I was going to," Jack said. "I have to admit, Cassie is pretty great."

"That was softball," Gus said, giving Jack a playful shove. "Time for some old-fashioned hardball. Go grab a bat."

As always, Coach started off pitching BP. Jack struggled with his timing at first. He kept telling himself that was to be expected. He hadn't faced real live pitching—other than Cassie—since his one day of practice with the Rays before he quit.

One day when he and Teddy and Cassie were on the field at school, Teddy had offered to pitch to him, but Jack had said, "Not without a screen in front of you."

"What about me?" Cassie'd said.

Jack had smiled at her and said, "Your team needs you too much."

"I'm not afraid of you."

And Jack had said, "That is what I'm afraid of."

In the batter's box now he told himself to stop pressing, to relax, just let it happen. He told himself not to squeeze the bat, because no matter how good a hitter you usually were, nobody could hit a baseball properly doing that.

He'd completely missed the first three pitches, even though they were fastballs right down the middle, like Coach was trying to put the ball on a tee for him. At least he got a small piece of the fourth pitch, fouling the ball back.

"Stop lunging," he muttered to himself under his breath, stepping out of the box, knowing the rest of the guys were probably watching him more closely right now than they ever had.

"I heard that," Coach called to him from the mound. "Couldn't have said it better myself."

Jack took in some air, let it out, took his stance, and tried to make his grip on the handle so light Gus could have walked over from the on-deck circle and taken the bat away from him with no problem.

Coach threw one more fastball over the middle of the plate, and this time Jack hit a line drive up the middle so hard that

Coach Leonard nearly had to dive to get out of the way.

"That is what I'm talkin' about," Gus said from behind him.

When Jack finished, knowing he'd gotten a lot more swings than the rest of the guys usually got, Coach asked if he wanted to do some pitching from the mound.

"Oh yeah," he said.

As he ran to get his glove, Gus yelled out to Coach, "Aren't you worried that it might affect his confidence when I start hitting bombs off him?"

"We'll just have to risk it," Coach said.

Scott was already in his full catching gear behind the plate. Coach handed Jack the ball and said, "Go easy."

Jack grinned and said, "Not gonna lie, Coach. Going easy today is gonna be hard."

He knew, just from the throwing he'd done already, that his arm felt good. After a half-dozen warm-up pitches, Scott threw the ball back to him hard and said, "We good?"

"Like they sing at Fenway when they sing 'Sweet Caroline,'" Jack said. "So good, so good, so good."

Gus got into the batter's box. Jack said, "This is batting practice. I am supposed to let you hit, you know."

"Not today," Gus said. "Knock yourself out trying to get me out."

It had been almost a year since Jack had tried to get somebody out, so he wondered if he would be able to get his fastball to behave. This was just BP, this wasn't a real game, but Gus's challenge, even issued in good fun, meant this was a competition between them now. All eyes were fixed on both of them. Mostly those eyes were on him, his teammates wanting to see what he had with a ball in his hand.

He wasn't going to overthrow, wasn't going to risk blowing out his arm before his season officially began. But he was feeling it now and he knew it, remembering how much he loved to compete.

Realizing how much he'd missed competing.

He went into his windup and promptly threw his first pitch over Gus's head and over Scott's head and all the way to the backstop on the fly.

Before anybody else could say anything, Jack couldn't help himself. He laughed.

"Sorry," he said to Gus after Scott retrieved the ball and threw it back to him. "For a second I thought they'd moved home plate over by the duck pond."

"Fear of the opposing hitter often does that to a guy," Gus said.

"You get six swings, right?" Jack said.

"Right."

"Let's see how many hits there are, and how many misses."

"Bring it."

Jack threw what he thought was a perfect pitch on the outside corner, but Gus went with it, lacing a clean single into leftfield.

One for him.

Jack came inside with the next pitch. Gus lined that one over T.W. Stanley's head at second base.

Two for him.

He stepped out of the box. Then he patted his mouth with the blue batting glove on his right hand, like he was stifling a yawn. "This is getting kind of boring," he said.

He was enjoying this.

"Don't worry, though," Gus said. "I can almost guarantee you're still going to make the team."

Jack knew something that Gus didn't know: He was really loose now and ready, really feeling it. Back in the middle of a baseball diamond, back in baseball, ball in his hand. He went into his motion again. This time he put a little something extra on the pitch. What the announcers liked to call giddyup. Gus had no chance, swinging right through the ball. It almost looked to Jack as if Gus didn't even start his swing until the ball was in Scott's mitt.

One for Jack.

He didn't say anything or try to show Gus up. He just smiled. Gus smiled back. They both knew this was pure baseball, even if they were the only ones keeping score.

Jack threw another fastball by him. The sound the ball made in the pocket of Scott's catcher's mitt . . . Jack knew he hadn't made that sound in a long time. Too long. But man, it sounded sweet.

Gus got him again on the next pitch, a fastball up, tomahawking the ball into centerfield. Jack watched it land, then turned and pointed to Gus. "Good lick," he said.

Three hits for Gus. Two misses. One more pitch. Scott set up low, telling Jack to put one at Gus's knees if he could. They both knew that Gus was a classic low-ball hitter, the way a lot of lefty hitters were. But Scott was doing what good catchers tried to do, changing the batter's eye level. Going low right after going high. Jack nodded.

The ball felt as if it exploded out of his hand, looking like it was coming in belt high and then just knifing into Scott's mitt, Scott barely having to move it. Gus swung and missed so hard he spun himself toward first base and nearly fell down.

From behind him Jack heard T.W. Stanley saying, "Wow, wow, wow."

Gus was the one pointing at Jack now.

"I think I missed you more than I just missed that pitch," he said.

"Missed you, too, brother."

Jack made a gesture with his glove that tried to take in their team, the whole field, everything. "Mostly I missed this," he said.

Coach came walking over to him and said, "Did I mention that you're starting Wednesday night?"

TWENTY-ONE

The Rays had an earlier practice the next night, five instead of six. When it was over, Jack stayed at the fields because the Orioles had a practice of their own at seven.

"You know," Cassie said when she got to Highland Park, "you don't have to help coach our team anymore now that you're back playing."

"Don't have to," Jack said. "Want to."

"Let me get this straight. You're going to practice with your own team, play games for your own team, and still be an assistant on my team?"

"Correction," Jack said. "Our team."

"Your parents are okay with all this baseball?"

"They were getting sick of having me around the house."

"I'm being serious," Cassie said.

"So am I. I told your dad I'd be his assistant coach, and I'm sticking with that. And the only time I'll miss one of your games is when I've got a game of my own."

"You really want to do this?"

"Hey," Jack said, "look at how well you're doing now that I'm around to give you pointers."

Her answer was a punch to the arm.

"Hey," Jack said, "that's my pitching arm."

"I forgot," Cassie said.

Cassie wasn't pitching tonight; she was at shortstop. She got three hits, made a great running catch on a pop-up to short center, then turned and threw out a runner at home on the same play, the girl dumb enough to run on her arm.

Play wasn't even close.

As soon as she got back to the bench, she came right over to where Jack was sitting.

"Must have been all those pointers that nailed Emma at the plate," she said.

Jack put up his hand for a high five. She tapped it with her glove.

"Were you, like, born this cocky?" Jack said.

"Just make sure you are tomorrow night," Cassie said.

"I'm not feeling very cocky," Jack said. "I haven't started a game since last season."

Cassie gave him one of her biggest smiles.

"No worries," she said. "I'll be there to help you."

The game was on the front field at Highland Park, one Jack had always thought had better lighting than the back fields.

"Tell me you don't think the lights are better here," Jack said to Gus before batting practice.

"You just think they're turned up tonight because you're pitching," Gus said.

"Yeah, that's me," Jack said, "always bringing my spotlight with me."

"Just as long as you bring your A game, too," Gus said. "'Cause you're gonna need it. We all are. These guys are good."

"These guys" were the White Sox, coming into the game with a 4–0 record, and everybody in the league knew that even before Jack had quit the team, they had just as good a chance to win the Atlantic and give themselves a chance at the Little League World Series as the Rays did. They were that good.

If Jack had been the best pitcher his age in the league last season, Nate Vinton—starting tonight for the White Sox—was the next best. He was a tall right-hander, tall enough to play center in basketball, with a fastball as big as he was.

He was also the White Sox's best hitter, and their best out-fielder, usually going out to left after he finished pitching. They also had a power guy behind him—Mike O'Keeffe, their catcher—and a centerfielder named Wayne Coffey, who Jack thought might be the fastest kid in their league.

The White Sox seemed to have just finished their own batting practice. But then Nate jumped into the box for a few extra swings against his dad, who coached the team. He hit shots to left and to right, asked for one more, and absolutely crushed one that disappeared over the centerfield fence. The ball ended up rolling into center on the field behind them, where the Mariners and Angels were finishing warm-ups.

"How lucky am I," Jack said, "getting to open up against such a soft opponent?"

"What, you thought this was going to be easy?" Gus said.

"Hope I'm ready for this."

"Now you're the one who sounds soft." Gus turned to face him on the bench and said, "Are you really worried? You?"

"My arm's fine," Jack said. "I just feel like I'm going from the first day of spring training straight to opening day."

"Guess what?" Gus said. "We all feel like this is opening day all over again. That's why we need to show these guys—and you need to show these guys—that when we've got you, we're still the best team in this stinking league."

He put out his fist. Jack bumped it. Scott Sutter came walking by and casually did the same thing. So did Gregg Leonard, and Hawk, and Andre, and T.W. Stanley. They had all practiced together for two nights as a team. But this was the real thing. This was a big game, even this early in the season, and they all knew it. And felt it.

Their team was their team again, Jack Callahan pitching and batting third.

He hit the ball hard in BP, spraying the ball all over the field even if he didn't jack one over the fence the way Nate Vinton had. When he was done, he ran out to short and fielded some ground balls, knowing he would be out there by the fourth inning. Coach Leonard had told him that even if his pitch count was stupidly low, he was only pitching three innings tonight.

"Even in Little League," Coach said, "it's a long season."

"I'm the guy who made it a little shorter for us," Jack said.

Coach put his arms on Jack's shoulders and turned him so they were facing each other.

"Son," he said, "I can't change things that happened in my life yesterday, or last week, and neither can you. And neither one of us should be worrying about what's going to happen tomorrow. All we can do is get after it tonight. Got that?"

"Got it."

"Take a look around this field and then ask yourself a question: Where else would you rather be?"

"Nowhere else," Jack said.

"Go out and play that way," Coach said. "Your whole life you've been hitting the catcher's glove. Just concentrate on doing that tonight, and everything else will take care of itself."

The Rays were the home team tonight, just by the way the schedule was written, the first game between them and the White Sox reading this way: *White Sox at Rays*. Next time they played, the White Sox would be the home team and bat last.

It meant Jack would get the ball first.

The Rays fans were on the first-base side of the field, behind their bench. Jack looked over and saw his mom and dad, sitting in the top row the way they always did. His dad preferred watching games from up there, as high up as he could be, so he could see more of the field from the top corner.

Jack waved at them. They waved back. Jack thought, *Finally we're all where we want to be.*

He was so focused on his parents that he didn't notice Cassie and Teddy at first, the two of them leaning over the wire fence separating the field from the bleachers.

"Were you going to say hello?" Cassie said.

"Well, excuse me for wanting to acknowledge my parents first," Jack said, grinning at her.

"I know," Cassie said. "I was just trying to lighten your vibe a little."

"Does my vibe need lightening?"

"Oh yes," Teddy said. "You've clearly taken the concept of 'game face' to a whole new level."

"What he's trying to say is smile, Callahan," Cassie said. "You've finally got a game of your own."

He shrugged and smiled. "Happy?" he said.

"Not as happy as you," she said, "whether you're showing it to us fans or not."

Then she reached over the fence with her fist. Jack touched it with his own.

"The only game," Cassie said, and she and Teddy went to take their seats.

He walked back to the Rays' bench. His teammates were waiting for him there. So was Coach Leonard.

"Have fun," he said. "Play hard. Don't show up your opponents, or the umps. Did I forget anything?"

"Win?" Gus said in a quiet voice.

Coach Leonard looked at Jack then and said, "How about you lead us out?"

Jack did that, sprinting to the mound, picking up the new baseball the ump had left sitting on the rubber, feeling the seams, rolling it around in his hand until he started rubbing it up. He stood with his back to home plate as he did, taking in the whole field. Somehow it looked bigger to him than usual. Maybe because the night felt so big to him. He kicked the rubber, knocking dirt out of his spikes. Then he began his warm-up pitches to Scott Sutter, throwing loose and easy, picking it up, putting some steam on the ball for his last few pitches. He pretended the game had already started. The ball in Scott's mitt sounded even louder and better than it had at practice, as distinctive to him as the crack of the bat.

After the last warm-up, Scott came out of his crouch and threw a strike down to second base. Brett Hawkins—playing short until Jack did—gloved the ball and put a tag on an imaginary runner.

The infielders threw the ball around. Jack took one more look up into the stands. He had thought a lot about his brother today and thought about him now. He pictured Brad sitting where he always used to sit, next to their mom.

Tonight the seat belonged to Mrs. Morales.

Gus ended up with the ball. He walked it over to Jack. Nobody had to tell Gus Morales to smile in that moment.

He stuffed the ball, hard, into the pocket of Jack's Pedroia.

"Let's do this," he said.

"Let's," Jack said.

Then he proceeded to walk the first batter he faced on four pitches, not one of them close to the strike zone.

Jack knew why, knew he was too amped up, overthrowing like crazy, unable to calm himself down. All that. As the batter—the White Sox shortstop, Conor Freeman—jogged down to first, Scott came about halfway to the mound before he threw the ball back to Jack. After he did, he made a calming gesture with his hands.

"Throw me a strike," Scott said. "I'll pay you."

Jack forced a smile and nodded.

He did throw strike one to the next batter, Wayne Coffey, who was taking all the way. Jack took a deep breath, let it out, and told himself the game was starting for him right here, even with a runner on first base.

Then came four more balls: One wild high, one in the dirt, and the next two outside, way outside. Scott somehow managed to make great backhand stops on both of them.

First and second, nobody out.

Coach called time, jogged out to the mound, took the ball out of Jack's glove, and rubbed it up, smiling from ear to ear.

"I think we clocked a couple of those fastballs at nine thousand miles an hour," he said. "You think maybe you could dial it down a little?"

"I'll try."

"And please remember my first rule of baseball," Coach said.

"Have fun," Jack said.

"Even when you're not having any fun at all."

Jack threw two quick strikes to Nate Vinton. Next he tried to get him to chase a ball intended to be way outside. But Nate was too smart. And too patient. He wasn't going to get himself out.

Jack went outside again.

Again Nate didn't bite.

Two and two.

In the past Jack had always prided himself on his control, even when he was trying to bust his best fastball past a hitter. But he knew he didn't have his normal control right now, not even close, even if he'd put some pitches to Nate where he wanted them.

Scott set up inside this time. Jack tried to get the ball inside. Just not enough.

The ball caught too much of the plate, and Nate Vinton was all over it. And as soon as Jack heard the sound of the bat on the ball—the same sound he'd heard when Nate had hit the ball to the next field in batting practice—he knew. If you were a pitcher, you always knew.

Jack turned and watched the same flight of the ball he'd seen when Nate had been hitting against his dad, saw the ball clear the centerfield fence with even more room to spare this time.

Just like that, after just three batters, it was 3–0, White Sox.

Coach was right about one thing, Jack thought.

It was a long season already.

TWENTY-TWO

This time it was Gus's turn to call time and come over to the mound. Jack was wondering who was next, his mom and dad?

"You got this," Gus said.

"What I've got," Jack said, "is nothing."

Gus said, "If they can score off you, we can score off Nate. Just get out of this inning and we'll figure it out."

"I'm the one who needs to figure it out," Jack said.

"So do it and stop acting like the game is over," Gus said. "It just started."

He ran back to first. Jack got out of the inning. It wasn't easy. He struck out O'Keeffe, who was swinging for the fences himself, and basically striking himself out on a ball up in his eyes. Then came an error by Hawk, a bloop single, two more men on. But T.W. saved Jack before things got any worse, making a diving stop on a line drive to his left, and doubling up the kid on first.

Jack dropped his glove on the bench, making it clear he didn't want to talk to anybody right now. He walked over to the drinking fountain near the fence, even though he'd brought Gatorade with him. He just wanted to be alone right now.

But Cassie was waiting for him.

"I can't handle another pep talk," he said.

"Not here to give you one."

"So you just happened to be thirsty when I was thirsty?"

"Nope." She shook her head. "I just wanted to tell you that you should keep pitching from the stretch. Even though the last guy tagged that last pitch, I thought you threw better from the stretch after Nate hit his home run."

"For real?"

"It seemed to slow you down," she said. "And you stopped walking guys."

"You think that will work?"

"I know it will," Cassie said. "Oh yeah, look at me. Now I'm coaching you!"

She ran back to sit with Teddy. When it was Jack's turn to hit, Gregg Leonard had just tripled past the centerfielder and was standing on third with one out.

Gus came over to stand with Jack in the on-deck circle. He tapped Jack's bat with his own. Then he grinned at him.

"You, like, can still hit, right?" he said.

"We're gonna find out."

He swung and missed at the first pitch Nate threw him. He thought he'd got all of the next one but caught the ball just an inch too close to the end of the bat, maybe less. And so what could have been a home run his first time up became a long sacrifice fly to center. He'd made an out but knew it was a good out, one that had scored a run for the Rays. He was on the board and so were they.

Gus doubled to right but never made it past second base. The game stayed 3–1. Jack went out to pitch the top of the second, and it turned out Cassie was right about pitching from the stretch, even with nobody on base. He got two quick outs and looked like he'd pitch a one-two-three inning, when Wayne Coffey hit what looked like a routine ground ball to Hawk at short.

But the ball went through Hawk's legs. Jack made what he thought was a great pitch to Nate Vinton, but he hit this little flare to right, just out of T.W.'s reach. Wayne went to third. First and third, two outs.

Nate took off for second with Mike O'Keeffe at the plate. Scott should have just let him have the stolen base. But he loved his arm and thought he could throw him out. Nate beat Hawk's tag. Wayne Coffey had been running from third as soon as the ball was in the air. Hawk tried to get him at home, but Wayne scored easily. Nate took third. The White Sox leftfielder dropped down a perfect bunt in front of Gus, Nate scored, and it was 5–1 before Jack finally got the third out.

Hawk caught up with Jack as he was coming off the field.

"Dude," Hawk said, "those runs are definitely on me. That should have been an easy inning."

"Forget it," Jack said. "Nobody stopped me from getting the last out." He turned as they crossed the baseline. "But, Hawk? I am not giving up another stinking run."

He didn't, putting down the White Sox in order in the third, putting the ball where he wanted to, wishing he'd started the game with this kind of fastball and this kind of location. In the bottom of the inning he got his first hit of the season, a clean single to left, scoring T.W. Gus followed that by hitting a Nate Vinton fastball off the wall in left, maybe a foot from being a home run. Jack could have walked home. It was 5–3. Scott Sutter singled Gus home, and now it was 5–4.

"Game on," Jack said when Gus got back to the bench.

He went out to shortstop for the top of the fourth. Now he didn't have to control every pitch, just the area between second and third. Andre Williams came on in relief, Coach telling him he needed two innings before he was going to give the ball to Jerry York, their closer, for the sixth.

"The plan," Coach said, "is for us to have the lead by then so Jerry actually has a game to close."

Andre got through his two innings, giving up just one hit. But the White Sox reliever, Danny Hayes, pitched two scoreless innings himself. The game was still 5–4, White Sox. Jerry came in from rightfield to strike out the side in the top of the sixth.

Last ups for the Rays, against the White Sox closer, Johnny Gaudreau, who'd been Jack's and Gus's teammate last season and was a left-hander with nasty stuff.

Or "filthy," as Gus called it.

Jerry York, batting eighth, was leading off for the Rays, followed by Andre. Then came the top of the order. The math was pretty simple, Jack knew. He needed two guys to get on if he was even going to get to the plate against Johnny Gaudreau.

Then Jerry struck out. So did Andre.

"Not the way I wanted the inning to start," Jack said to Gus.

"Hey," Gus said, "we've been in bad spots before and come back, right?"

Jack thought about where he'd been a week ago and said, "Right."

Somehow T.W. worked a walk out of Johnny Gaudreau, laying off a three-two pitch that Jack was afraid was going to be called strike three but got called a ball. Gregg Leonard hit the first pitch he saw over third base. Jack thought it might be a double at first, but Nate Vinton—now playing left—quickly closed on the ball and held T.W. at second.

So the night, Jack's first night of baseball, had come down to him.

He walked around the ump and Mike O'Keeffe, the White Sox catcher. He took a couple of practice swings and then gave a quick look over at the stands. But his eyes stopped on Cassie, by herself, leaning over the fence near the water fountain.

She just gave a single nod of her head.

Then smiled.

Jack put his head down as he took his stance, because he felt himself smiling too. In that moment he knew, win or lose, that the feeling he had right now was what he had missed most of all, whether he got a hit or made the last out of the game.

It wasn't just one thing, it was everything: being excited, being nervous, even being a little scared.

This wasn't just baseball. It was sports. It was why you played, for a moment like this. It was just better in baseball.

You against the pitcher. As if the two of you were playing for the championship of the next few pitches.

Jack dug in with his back foot. Set his hands. Waited.

Johnny threw his best fastball. Jack thought he was on it, but his timing was a bit off, and he fouled it back.

0–1.

Jack laid off the next pitch, sure it was outside. The home plate ump thought differently, deciding it had caught the outside corner even though Jack, who'd always had such a great batter's eye, knew it hadn't.

0–2.

Just like that, he was in a hole, one strike away from the game being over, from the White Sox staying undefeated and the Rays falling into a 1–4 hole and probably into last place.

Jack stepped out. He wasn't facing Cassie in a girls' softball practice. But he knew Johnny, and he knew Johnny wanted to have his hero moment now and strike Jack out on three pitches to end the game.

He just knew Johnny was going to come right at him. And he did, with the hardest pitch he'd thrown yet to Jack and in the inning, a rising fastball that TV announcers liked to say was "letter high."

Jack was ready for it.

At first he thought he was too ready, that he'd been too

quick, pulled the ball too much, done nothing more than hit a screaming foul ball past third.

But he hadn't.

The ball landed about a foot fair and ran toward the left-field corner, and by the time Nate Vinton ran it down, Gregg Leonard had chased T.W. across home plate and it was Rays 6, White Sox 5.

Now Jack was back.

TWENTY-THREE

There was no school on Friday because of a teachers' work day.

Not only was there no school, there was no baseball practice later for either the Rays or the Orioles, and no games. So just like that it had turned into a summer day, and Jack had decided it was the right day for Cassie and Gus to officially make up.

It wasn't like they were still going at each other the way they had that day in the cafeteria. Things seemed to be cool between them at school and when Gus would show up for one of his sister's games or Cassie would show up for a Rays game, now that Jack was back playing.

But they had never hung out together. Jack knew from Cassie that they had never talked about what had been said that day at school, and he wanted everybody to move past that for good, now that things were going better for all of them.

Cassie had talked about Jack and Teddy meeting her at the pond. When he suggested that Gus come along, she said, "Why?"

"Because he's my friend and you're my friend, and I want you guys to be friends."

"We're not *not* friends," she said. "Can't you be happy with that?"

"No," he said.

"'Course not," she said. "You give a mouse a cookie, he wants a piece of cake."

"Strawberry shortcake," he said.

"Fine," she said.

They all met up at Jack's house, so they could walk to the pond together. Gus and Cassie showed up first. While they were waiting for Teddy, Cassie was the one who took the lead.

"Listen," she said to Gus, "I'm sorry I was so hard on you that day at lunch after Jack quit the team."

"No worries," Gus said, and seemed willing to leave it at that until Jack poked him with an elbow.

"What?" Gus said.

"Isn't there something you want to add?"

Gus said to Cassie, "Sorry I was such a jerk."

Cassie nodded. "Yeah, you were."

She put out a fist. Gus bumped it with his own. "Friends?" Cassie said.

"Yeah," Gus said, "and I'll tell you why."

"Why?" Cassie said.

"Because I never want to get on your bad side ever again!" Gus said.

They all laughed. When they stopped, Cassie looked at Jack and said, "I take it back. He's not an idiot after all."

"I'll try not to be one today," Gus said.

"Good," Cassie said. "Because if you are an idiot, I hope you're a good swimmer."

When Teddy got there and they were walking toward the pond, Gus whispered to Jack, "She still scares me."

"Join the club," Jack said.

"I heard that," Cassie said.

A few minutes later they were sitting on the Connorses' dock, taking in the sun, nowhere else any of them needed to be for the rest of the afternoon.

THE ONLY GAME

Jack had been so busy with baseball he'd forgotten how much fun it was to do nothing, even though he had suggested earlier that they go over to Highland Park or even school later to play ball.

But Gus Morales, who always wanted to play baseball, even in the middle of winter, torched the idea.

"I'm just exercising my mind today," he said, "and giving my body the day off."

Cassie grinned. "That's going to be a pretty short workout. Just throwing that out there."

"I'm deeper than you think," Gus said.

"He's got a lot of layers," Jack said.

"Yeah," Teddy said. "Somewhat like an onion."

Teddy got to his feet, picked a rock out of the pile they'd collected, and made a pretty impressive throw into the trees on their right. Then he sat right back down.

"There, Jack," he said. "Now I got my throwing in for the day, so we don't have to work out later."

Cassie got up now and challenged Jack to a rock-skipping contest, most skips won. She blew him away on her first throw, so many skips that Jack lost count. Jack's throw wasn't even close.

"Best two out of three?" he said to her.

Before she could answer, Teddy said, "Do you guys ever stop competing?"

Jack looked at Cassie. They both looked at Gus. All of them said, "Nah."

"It's the jock thing," Teddy said. "I'm never gonna get the jock thing."

"Yeah, you will," Jack said. "You're becoming one yourself, you just don't know it yet."

"No, I am getting into shape. And that's pretty much because you haven't given me a choice."

They had worked out the day before after school, at Jack's house. There was some basic baseball stuff at first, Jack pitching and Teddy in a catcher's crouch. The more they did this, the more Jack started to get the idea that Teddy really could be a catcher next season if he wanted to. After that they switched to football, Teddy having confided in Jack that if he ever did get interested in trying to make a team, it would be football next fall.

But he made it clear that Jack was not allowed to tell another living soul.

Jack had set up some lawn chairs around the yard and made Teddy run some agility drills around them, even when Jack would throw him the ball and tell him to pretend he was a broken-field runner and the chairs were guys trying to tackle him.

After they'd finished that, Jack even convinced Teddy to go on a one-mile run around his neighborhood.

"I have to run even though I'm not being chased?" Teddy had said. "Well, that makes zero sense."

"You'll feel better when we're finished," Jack had said. "You always feel better at the end of the workout."

"No, I just feel more tired."

It was important to Jack that he keep working out with Teddy, because it was a way for him to continue to show Teddy that they were friends.

Teddy hadn't come right out and asked Jack if they really were friends. But he had made a few comments, trying to keep them funny, about how Jack didn't need him anymore now that he was playing ball again, and Jack could feel free to call off the workouts anytime he wanted to. And it was why Jack had included him in today's plan, even though there was no real plan beyond just hanging out.

On the dock now, Cassie jumped up and said, "Let's go for a walk. I'm bored."

Jack couldn't tell whether it was Teddy or Gus groaning the loudest. Maybe it was just the same loud, sad sound coming out of both of them at the same time.

"There's no school today," Teddy said. "Nobody rang a bell. We don't have to get to our next period."

"Or activity," Gus said.

Jack, though, knew better than to go against Cassie.

"Where to?" he said.

"We'll just go exploring!" Cassie said.

"Jocks," Teddy said, and let Jack pull him up, resigned to his fate.

It really did feel like a summer day, all of them in shorts. Cassie led the way, of course. They were taking a different path through the woods than she and Jack had ever taken before, winding their way in and out of sunlight. Cassie said this was a path that runners used, or people walking their dogs. Sometimes they'd go long periods without talking, the only noises the slap of their sneakers on the path, or one of them occasionally snapping a twig.

"You know your way around back here even better than I knew," Jack said to Cassie at one point.

"I'm like a human GPS system."

"The GPS woman in my mom's car is nicer."

"Nicer than me?" Cassie said.

"You plan on telling us where we're going?" Gus said.

Jack had a feeling they were going to end up where they always did, at the falls, but he knew better than to ruin Cassie's surprise.

"You'll find out soon enough," she said.

And they did. They had taken a different route today for sure, but as they got closer to Small Falls, Jack felt them walking more and more uphill, almost like they were making their way up a steep flight of stairs. Finally he heard the sound of the water, and they were coming out into the clearing, over here on their side of the Walton River. The old bridge that took you over to the east side was swaying slightly in the afternoon breeze.

"C'mon," Cassie said, "there's this cool rock formation on the other side that I haven't even shown Jack yet. I've been saving it."

"If I'd known this was where you were taking us, I would've run here," Gus said. "I love this place! Angela and I used to come up here all the time with my dad."

"I wouldn't say I love it, exactly," Jack said. "The first time I ever crossed the bridge, I felt like one of those tightrope walkers."

"Oh, don't be a wuss," Cassie said. "My dad says that bridge has been around for fifty years. You just can't fool around going across, because it does feel a little shaky sometimes when there's a lot of people crossing at the same time."

She started across the bridge, Gus with her, Jack a few feet behind. Cassie and Gus were talking away, laughing, whatever awkwardness they'd felt at Jack's house gone now. They were walking quickly across the bridge as casually as walking across the street before the light changed.

Jack heard Cassie say to Gus, "Want to race?"

"Bring it," Gus said.

"Wait!" Jack said.

He was only a few yards onto the bridge, hanging back from them, holding on to the railing.

"C'mon, don't run," he said.

"Why not?" Cassie said. "It'll be awesome!"

"Not for me," Jack said.

"I just told you this old thing is safe," Cassie said. "I'll even prove it to you."

She started jumping up and down like it was a trampoline, making the bridge shake.

"Cass," he said, "cut it out."

"For the last time," she said, "stop being a wuss." But she was smiling at him.

"Not being one."

"Fine, you go ahead and walk. Gus and I will run," she said. She pointed behind Jack and said, "But you better tell Teddy to pick up the pace a little."

That was when Jack turned and saw that Teddy wasn't on the bridge.

TWENTY-FOUR

All Jack could think of when he saw Teddy there, frozen in place, was the kid that the other guys used to pick on in gym class until Jack had finally made them stop.

He looked like he'd gone back to being Teddy Bear.

"I'll wait for you," Jack said. "We'll let them have their fun."

Teddy shook his head.

"I'm good," he said.

He didn't look good.

Behind him Jack heard Gus say, "C'mon, Teddy, we were just messing around. It's totally cool out here."

Then Gus was the one jumping up and down the way Cassie just had.

"Please stop," Teddy said in a voice barely loud enough to be heard over the sound of the water below them.

He looked more frightened than ever. And he still hadn't moved.

"Gus, please cut it out," Jack said. "Both of you cut it out."

Cassie smiled at Teddy. "You've really never been out here before?" she said to him.

He shook his head.

"Well, then you gotta come and see the view," she said. "It's killer."

"If I'd known this was where we were headed, I never would have come at all," Teddy said.

"Listen, we'll all walk across together," Gus said. He couldn't keep the grin off his face or hide how much fun he was having being up there. "I promise not to bolt, even though you know I want to."

In that moment Jack realized he knew that look on Gus's face. This was the same excited look Brad would have on his face when he was describing to Jack some daredevil thing he'd done. Or when he was on the diving board, getting ready to show Jack one of his crazy flips.

Jack turned to Gus and Cassie and said, "This is a bad idea."

"Let me go talk to him," Cassie said.

"No," Jack said. "If he doesn't want to come out here, he shouldn't. If you guys want to keep going, we'll meet you back on the dock."

"You sure?" Cassie said.

Jack said, "If I can get him to change his mind, we'll meet you on the other side in a little while."

But when he started walking back, Teddy was the one who bolted.

"Let him go," Cassie said.

"I can't," Jack said. "He was there for me when I needed him. I have to be there for him."

"Then we'll all go," Gus said.

Jack thought it would be easy for them to catch up with Teddy, even if he was in much better running shape now than he used to be. But as Cassie had shown them on the way up here, there were a lot of paths in these woods, and Teddy could have taken any of them back to the pond.

"I really am an idiot," Cassie said.

"There was no way you could've known he was afraid of

heights," Jack said. "I've been spending more time with him than anybody, and I didn't know."

They had made their way back to the dock, just to see if Teddy was there. He wasn't. Now they were walking back to Cassie's house, where Jack and Gus had left their bikes.

"This is bad," Jack said.

"He's Teddy," Cassie said. "By tomorrow he'll be making a joke out of the whole thing."

But Jack couldn't forget the look on Teddy's face he'd seen when he turned around on the bridge.

"He was starting to get some confidence," Jack said. "Now this has to happen."

"Jack, you just said this wasn't Cassie's fault," Gus said. "But guess what? It's not yours, either."

"Either way, I gotta find him."

He tried Teddy's phone, but it went straight to voice mail. He'd probably turned it off. Then Jack tried calling his house, but all he got there was the answering machine, the voice of Teddy's mom saying that if it was an emergency to try her cell, or call her at her real estate office.

"Nothing," Jack said.

He got on his bike and said he'd call them later, after he talked to Teddy.

"Immediately," Cassie said. "And tell him I'm sorry."

"I will," he said, and headed in the direction of Teddy's house. Just because he wasn't answering the phone didn't mean he wasn't there.

I gotta find him.

It was like Jack had told Teddy Madden:

Sometimes people didn't know when they needed to be helped.

Jack took a brief detour first and rode into town. He went up and down the streets of Walton's small downtown area. He checked the pizza place and the ice cream store and Starbucks. He even stopped at the Walton Public Library, because another of Teddy's secrets—Brad wasn't the only one who'd told Jack secrets—was that he loved finding a quiet spot in the stacks and reading. Nobody their age that Jack knew loved reading as much as Teddy Madden did.

But he wasn't at the library.

Jack tried calling him again. Still no answer. Now he rode to Teddy's house, rang the front doorbell, and waited. No answer to that, either. He thought Teddy might just be inside, still wanting to be left alone. But something about the house, even standing outside it, made Jack feel as if it was empty.

He walked back down their front walk to where he'd left his bike leaning against their mailbox.

Out loud he said, "Where you at?"

It was the way Teddy always texted him:

WHERE U AT?

In that moment, Jack knew where he was at. He didn't know why he knew. But he did.

Teddy was alone in the dugout behind Walton Middle School, the same place he and Jack had sat the day Jack told him about Brad, and why he'd quit the Rays. He was in the same corner of the dugout where Cassie had found them.

Teddy didn't look at all surprised when he looked up and saw Jack standing there.

"Wow," he said. "You're a private detective, too."

"I'm your friend."

"I don't want to talk about it."

Jack sat down on the steps across from him. "Wait a second. I thought you said not talking about stuff wasn't allowed."

"There's nothing to talk about," Teddy said.

"Yeah, there is."

"Look at it this way, Jack," he said. "Once a Teddy Bear, always a Teddy Bear."

"You know that's not true."

"I was a big baby," Teddy said. "Like, a *really* big baby."

"No, you weren't. Everybody's afraid of something. I wish my brother had been. I remember one time a bat got into our house, and bats have scared me silly ever since."

Somehow that got a laugh out of Teddy. "Least that doesn't include baseball bats."

"You laugh," Jack said. "But you should have heard that thing flapping around until my dad knocked it down with a broom and we got it into a garbage bag and let it go."

"It's almost as funny as this joke," Teddy said. "Why didn't the chicken cross the bridge? Because he was too scared to get to the other side."

"You're making this way worse than it was."

"It's like I keep trying to tell you," Teddy said. "I'm not like you guys. Even a walk in the woods turns into a competition. So you guys won, I lost."

Then he looked up and said to Jack, "You don't have to be here. You don't have to be with me, period."

Finally he'd come right out with it, what Jack knew he'd been thinking.

"I hang out with you because I want to hang out with you," Jack said.

"You don't have to treat me like some kind of charity case anymore," Teddy said. "You'd be doing me a favor, because then

I wouldn't have to keep pretending that I like working out."

"That's a lie."

"Wow," Teddy said. "This is some great day. First I was a coward at the falls, now I'm a liar, too."

"You're usually the one who does most of the talking," Jack said. "Can I talk for a minute without you interrupting me?"

"What choice do I have? If I try to leave, you'll probably turn this into one of your tackling drills."

"I want you to admit that you do like working out, no matter how many jokes you make about it," Jack said. "I see you when you're getting after it. I see the look on your face. I know how good you feel when we're done."

"Fine!" Teddy said. "I do like it! And I do like the way it makes me feel, mostly about myself. Are you happy?"

Jack smiled. "Very," he said.

"It still doesn't mean I'm ever going to be any good."

"May I talk again?"

Teddy put up his hands in surrender.

"You think you know me so well now?" Jack said. "Well, I've gotten to know you. I can see how much you like football. And you know what else? If we'd started working on your baseball skills a few months ago, you'd be catching for some team by now."

Teddy said, "Sometimes I get tired just listening to you. How do you have this much energy?"

"I saved up a lot when I wasn't playing baseball."

"But now you are playing again," Teddy said. "And you're still helping coach Cassie's team. You've got enough to do without wasting time on me."

"Okay, now I'm the one getting tired of listening to you."

"I have that effect on people."

"Shut up."

That got a smile out of him. "Shutting up is hard for me," Teddy said.

"Tell me about it," Jack said.

They both laughed. It was late afternoon by now. Jack had made sure to call his mom before he'd left town and tell her what had happened at Small Falls. His mom had said, "If you do find him, tell him that being afraid of heights is a part of who he is. But not all he is."

"You're really smart," Jack had told her.

"There's this test we have to pass before they allow us to have children."

In the dugout now he told Teddy what his mom had said, word for word.

"I don't care about being afraid of heights as much as I care that I was afraid in front of you guys."

He looked hard at Jack, who saw how red his eyes were, as if he'd been crying before Jack got there.

"Are you serious? We felt worse than you did. Even Cassie."

"Now you're just making stuff up."

"When did you ever hear her admit she'd made a mistake about anything?" Jack said.

What came out of Teddy then came out as a whisper.

"I wish I could have crossed that bridge," he said.

"So you will next time."

"Don't be so sure," Teddy said.

"I've been trying to tell you," Jack said. "I've got more confidence in you than you have in yourself."

Teddy said, "Thanks for coming to find me."

"You would have done the same."

"Nah," Teddy said. "Too much work."

"Wait a second!" Jack said. "Did somebody say work?"

Teddy put his head down in mock agony. "Oh no. What have I done?"

"Baseball or football?"

"Football."

Teddy went home and got the new ball his mom had bought for him. They played until it was time for Jack to go home for supper, and for once, it was Teddy who wanted to keep going. Jack was the one who did get tired this time, because Teddy was playing quarterback, showing off his arm, and Jack was the one running one pass pattern after another.

On the ride home, Jack was still thinking about everything that had happened today. Thinking how Teddy really wasn't so different from him and Cassie and Gus.

Thinking that Teddy was turning into more of a jock, a little bit at a time, than he realized.

What he'd shown Jack today was that when he went down— the way he'd gone down in gym class that time—he could get back up.

All Jack had done was give him a hand.

A little help.

TWENTY-FIVE

There was something different about Teddy the next couple of weeks. He was still the same funny guy. Jack just didn't think he was trying to be as funny all the time. Teddy was quieter than when they'd first started hanging around, even when it was only the two of them.

Jack didn't bring up what had happened at the bridge, and neither did Teddy. Cassie had tried to talk about it with him one time when they were all having pizza in town, because nothing was off-limits with her. But Teddy finally told her to please stop trying to put a smiley face on what had happened.

"I know you feel bad that you took me there," he said. "But you make me feel worse every time you talk about it, like I'm standing there watching you guys all over again. Okay?"

"Okay," she said.

Jack and Teddy kept working out, every chance Jack got around his baseball schedule and Cassie's softball schedule. Teddy kept showing up at Rays games, and even Cassie's games sometimes. Jack and Teddy would text at night, and talk on the phone. There was no question, with either of them, that they really were friends now. And Teddy seemed just as comfortable when Cassie and Gus were part of the pack.

And none of that was the big news in Jack's life. The big news was that nobody could beat the Rays, who had climbed out of last place and begun to move up the standings. They'd become the team everybody had expected them to be at the start of the season.

They'd played six games since Jack started to play again and won them all. After his first sketchy start against the White Sox, Jack had dominated in his next two, giving up a grand total of one run in seven innings. Coach Leonard let him go four innings his last time out against the Tigers because his pitch count was so low.

MIKE LUPICA

Suddenly the Rays were 7–3 with four games left in the regular season, and only the White Sox and Mariners, both at 8–2, had better records. And the Rays were playing the Mariners tonight on the back field at Highland Park, with a chance to tie them for second place.

Four teams in the Atlantic made the play-offs. Before the game, Gus was talking about what he had been talking about a lot lately, getting into first place and getting the top seed for the play-offs.

"Let's just get into the play-offs first and then worry about seedings," Jack said. "It's not like if we don't end up first we have to go on the road."

Gus shook his head, as if he simply couldn't believe how dense his friend was.

"If it comes down to the last inning of the championship game," he said, "I want us to have last ups. And so do you."

"Gotta admit," Jack said, "you're right."

"The season didn't start the way it was supposed to," Gus said. "But it's going to end that way. Winning the Atlantic is the first step to us punching our ticket to the World Series."

"How about we just focus on winning the game tonight?"

"I like the Rays' chances," Gus said. "I hear their starting pitcher doesn't stink."

Jack left Gus then and walked down the rightfield line. He

THE ONLY GAME

sat down in the grass, his back against the place where the wire fence ended and the green rightfield wall, the one with all the local advertisements on it, began. He had done this the last couple of starts, just spent time alone for a few minutes to get ready for the game.

His dad was big on treating every pitch and every at bat of the game the same. He believed that if you could do that, if you had the same routine whether it was the top of the first inning or the bottom of the last, you took pressure off yourself.

"It's about process, not worrying about results," Tim Callahan said. "You know how much I love golf, at least when I don't hate it. Watch the pros on TV. It's why they have the same routine before every shot."

Jack thought about that now, closed his eyes and pictured himself on the mound tonight in the top of the first, imagining himself throwing strike one.

But he was also thinking about Brad.

Even with the season going as well as it was, there were times when he missed his brother as much as he ever had.

Sometimes more.

As much as he loved sharing the success he was having right now with his teammates, as much as he loved sharing it with his parents and his friends, he still wanted to be sharing it with his brother.

The brother who'd found a way to get him the Pedroia ball and who'd written him that note.

He pulled the note out now, angling his body so nobody could see what he was doing or would want to ask him later what he was reading in the outfield.

Then he read it all over again.

It wasn't the original. The original was in the top drawer of his desk. This was a copy he'd made on his printer, one he carried in his back pocket to every game.

I love watching you play. Always have, always will.

He didn't have to read all of it, didn't really need to read it at all. He pretty much had Brad's words memorized by now. He still carried the words with him to his games. It was as much a good luck charm for him as the Pedroia ball sitting in its stand on top of his dresser.

This way he could bring Brad to the games with him.

He wasn't sad all the time. He didn't go through his days feeling sorry for himself. More than ever, he knew how happy baseball made him, how important it was to him. He was smart enough about himself to know he wasn't really himself when he didn't have a ball game to play, or one to look forward to, when he wasn't part of a team.

He'd tried to explain all that to his dad when they were sitting in the parking lot, before Jack had gotten out of the car, how he felt happy and sad at the same time.

"I feel the exact same way," his dad had said. "The trick for all of us is to find a way for happy to win."

"It's hard sometimes."

His dad laughed. "No," he'd said, "it's impossible sometimes. But the thing I try to focus on, the thing I hold on to, is how happy your brother was in the short time we all had him in our lives. And I tell myself that the only thing that would have made him sad was if we weren't living happy lives without him. Starting with you."

Then he'd pulled Jack toward him and kissed him on the forehead and said, "Now go play the way you can and make yourself happy."

"Process, not results."

"There you go."

Jack put the note back in his pocket and walked back to join his teammates. The Rays were the home team tonight. It meant Jack got the ball in the top of the first.

He struck out the side.

He did the same thing in the top of the second.

The Rays were already ahead 3–0 by then. When Jack tripled home two more runs in the bottom of the inning, it was 5–0, then 7–0 after Gus hit a home run over the leftfield wall.

He went to the mound in the top of the third and struck out the side again. Nine up, nine down. Six of the Mariners' hitters had gone down swinging. Three had taken called third strikes. He'd never gone through the batting order like this in his life.

It wasn't a perfect game. He'd only pitched three innings. But it felt pretty perfect. Jack was ready to keep going, to see if he could keep his streak alive, but when he got back to the bench after the top of the third, Coach told him he was done for the night.

"We don't need to rub it in," Coach said. "And we might face these guys in the play-offs. Let them just remember the way you punched them all out. You good with that?"

Jack grinned at Coach and said, "Somebody's always telling me it's a long season."

He sat down and drank some Gatorade. Gus came over and sat down next to him.

"You want to know how many pitches you threw outside the strike zone?" Gus said.

"How many?"

"Eight," he said. "To nine batters. I just asked Mr. Sutter."

Scott's dad kept the score book.

"As soon as Scott threw me the ball back," Jack said, "I was ready to go."

He was still pitching out of the stretch, he'd stayed with that after his first start. But he felt like he could have had the biggest windup and leg kick in the world and still have kept hitting Scott's mitt tonight, putting the ball where he wanted to. Not thinking—or overthinking, the way he had in his first start.

Just getting out of his own way and pitching.

He was still two batters away from getting a chance to hit in the bottom of the third, when he heard Cassie yell, "Hey."

She was leaning over the fence. She'd come to the game with Teddy, but he was nowhere in sight. When Jack asked where he was, Cassie said, "He lost interest when he found out you weren't getting to pitch anymore."

"Can't lie, Cass," Jack said, "that was fun tonight."

"Even I never struck out nine batters in a row," she said.

"You sound a little jealous," Jack said. "Is something like that even possible for Cassie Bennett?"

"No," she said.

But as she was walking back to the bleachers, she looked back over her shoulder, grinning, and said, "Maybe a little bit."

Jack looked to the top of the stands then and waved up at his parents. They waved back, his mom pumping her fist like a complete maniac. On this night, she was the one who looked happiest of all.

MIKE LUPICA

Tonight, Jack noticed, Mrs. Morales wasn't at the game, so the seat next to his mom, Brad's old seat, was empty.

Or maybe it wasn't.

Perfect night all the way around, until Jack's catcher broke his ankle.

TWENTY-SIX

t happened in the bottom of the fifth. The Rays were ahead
8–2 by then, and Scott was the only guy in the original lineup
who didn't have a hit.

But with one out he hit a loud line drive that seemed to split
the centerfielder and leftfielder and get past them almost before
either one of them broke on the ball.

Because Scott was a catcher and always taking heat from the
guys because of his lack of speed, you could see him busting it

out of the box, like he wanted to show everybody he had jets if he needed them.

By the time he rounded first, he could see that the center-fielder was just getting to the ball, a few feet short of the wall. Jack saw Scott put his head down now, sure he was thinking triple all the way.

Maybe it was because he was running with his head down when he got close to second base. Maybe he was slightly off stride. Or maybe it was just bad luck. But instead of cutting the inside of the bag, the way Coach Leonard had taught them, his left foot came down hard right on the top of second base.

Jack saw what they all saw in the next moment, saw Scott's left ankle collapse underneath him, saw him go down.

Even then he was a ballplayer, crawling back to put a hand on second, not wanting to get tagged out. He looked up at the field umpire and asked for time. Then he was curled up in the dirt, holding his ankle as Coach Leonard came running for him from the third-base coaching box and Scott's dad came running from the bench, his score book still in his hand.

They both knelt down next to him, Coach with his arm around him, talking to him, Scott nodding. Coach and Scott's dad carefully helped him to his feet. Or foot, because Scott had his left leg bent underneath him, only touching air.

They slowly walked him off. Players on both teams

applauded. They didn't even stop at the bench, kept walking right past it, to where Mr. Sutter's car was parked in the lot. The rest of the Rays watched from behind the bench as they lifted Scott into the backseat so he could stretch out. Coach closed the door. Mr. Sutter got behind the wheel and the car pulled away. Coach came back and told them they were on their way to Lewisboro Medical Center for X-rays.

The Rays scored three more runs the rest of the way and ended up winning 10–2. Nobody cared. By the end of the night they were all texting one another and Facebook-posting one another with the news that Scott's ankle was broken and that their first-string catcher—their only catcher, really—was lost for the season.

Gus's second-to-last text of the night to Jack read this way:

GUY WE CAN LEAST AFFORD TO LOSE
OTHER THAN U WE LOSE.

Jack's response:

U GOT THAT RIGHT.

Gus:

NOW WHAT?

Jack:

NO CLUE.

It was because he didn't have a clue. Good catchers were rare enough in their league. You were lucky to have one good one, much less two. Brett Hawkins was their emergency catcher, and Coach made sure to give him enough work during practice and would have put him into tonight's game sooner if he hadn't been rooting for Scott to get a hit.

But they all knew that their real backup catcher was nobody.

Now they needed a backup plan for that as they got ready to play their biggest games of the season, still as close to being in fifth place—and out of the play-offs—as they were to first, no matter how many games in a row they'd won.

What had started out as such a perfect night for Jack, striking out those nine guys in a row, had ended as badly as it could for him and for his team.

It wasn't as if he needed any more reminders about how fast and easy it was to go from happy to sad, in baseball and pretty much everything else.

But here it was for him again.

For all of them this time.

TWENTY-SEVEN

B rett said he'd be happy to catch the rest of the way if it helped the team, even if the last time he'd been a regular catcher was when he was nine.

Gus told Coach that he'd never caught in his life, but that he was a fast learner. "How hard is it to be a catcher, anyway?" he joked.

This was at practice two nights later, and Gus was only saying that for Scott's benefit, because Scott was there with the rest of the team even with his crutches and the soft cast on his left ankle.

"Either Brett or Gus would be fine, Coach," Scott said. "Especially Gus. After all, you told me they call catcher's equipment the tools of ignorance, right?"

Jack raised a hand.

"Can I try?" he said. "I know I could do it. And think about it: You could move Hawk to short full-time, since he already plays there when I'm pitching. We all know T.W. can play anywhere in the infield, and he could move to third. And Andre is always saying he's a born infielder."

Coach Leonard smiled when Jack was finished. "He pitches, he hits, he plays shortstop. Now he even coaches! Thanks for the offer, Jack. But no thanks. I'm not risking my best pitcher's right hand behind home plate."

He nodded at Hawk. "Suit up, big boy. You get first crack at this, since you're the one with the most practice."

To all of them he said, "We're going to be fine."

But Jack wondered about that after watching Hawk move around behind the plate and just try to do basic catching stuff over the next half hour. He'd never really paid much attention when Hawk filled in for Scott before. Tonight he did. And didn't like what he saw.

It might have been a simple case of nerves, but Hawk was having trouble even catching the ball in the pocket of the mitt Scott had loaned him. It kept happening even when Jack was on the mound, trying to lay the ball in there so that Hawk barely had to move the mitt.

When Coach told Jack to bounce a few in front of the plate, it was a total disaster. Hawk struggled to keep the ball in front of him, and most of the pitches just scooted through his legs and back to the screen.

None of it would have mattered if this were the first day of practice. It wasn't. They were a little over a week away from the end of the regular season, three games left, still not guaranteed a play-off spot even if they did still have an outside shot at first place.

Jack could see how hard Hawk was trying. But the more he struggled, the more he pressed. It only made his mechanics worse, if you could even call them mechanics. When Coach told him to make some throws to second, the ball either bounced six feet in front of the bag or sailed over T.W.'s head and into centerfield.

When he finally made a perfect throw to T.W., he raised both arms in the air in triumph, mocking himself.

"Coach," he said, "you think when guys are stealing I can make them keep going back to first and trying again till I get it right?"

"Hawk," Coach said, "I want you to stop being so hard on yourself. Scott's been catching his whole life. You just concentrate on catching the ball. If you're worried about guys stealing, hold the ball. It's not like even the best catchers in this league throw out a lot of guys."

"It's just that I feel like I'm learning baseball all over again."

"I'm not expecting you to be a great catcher," Coach said. "You're a good baseball player. Just be yourself."

"Yeah," Gus said from first. "A slow runner and a slow thinker."

Hawk said, "Look who's talking."

"Hey!" Gus said. "I am *not* a slow runner."

By the time practice was over, Hawk had shown some slight improvement. Coach called all his players around him.

"Gonna repeat this one more time: Hawk is gonna be fine, and we're gonna be fine. I know we lost Scott, and that's a huge loss. But the last time I checked, we hadn't lost a game in a long time."

Coach put out his hand. The Rays put their hands on top of it.

"Anybody else want to add something?" he said.

Jack was the one who spoke.

"Beat the Rockies," he said.

Their opponent the next night.

Then they were all jumping up and down, except for Scott, yelling, "Beat the Rockies!"

One more time Jack wondered what people who weren't a part of a team did to feel the way he did just then.

The Rockies had a 7–4 record, which meant they were only one game behind the Rays in the standings. Andre was starting for them. Coach had told him he might stretch him out to four innings if his pitch count was manageable, then go straight to Jerry York for the last two innings if they had the lead.

They didn't.

A lot of it was because of Hawk.

Not all of it, not even close. But this was one of those games when Andre struggled with his control, walking the first guy he faced in the top of the first. Jack had hoped they could avoid dealing with base runners in the first inning, for Hawk's sake.

The Rockies knew Scott was hurt even before they saw him on crutches. Every team with a shot at winning the Atlantic knew by now. So they didn't waste any time testing Hawk. Their leadoff man, Brian McAuley, took off on the first pitch. Hawk came out of his crouch and came up throwing, but bounced the throw as badly as he'd been bouncing them in practice. T.W. looked like a hockey goalie, blocking the ball with his right leg so it wouldn't go past him into centerfield and give Brian third base with nobody out.

The pitch had been a ball. Brian took off from second on the

MIKE LUPICA

very next pitch and would have stolen third easily, except that Andre hit the batter, Shemar Miller.

First and second, nobody out.

On the first pitch to their number three hitter, both Brian and Shemar took off on a pitch a foot outside. Hawk tried to make the shorter throw, to third. But the ball sailed over the head of Dan Neenan, in for Hawk at third, and rolled all the way into the leftfield corner. By the time the ball was back in the infield, both runners had scored. It was 2–0, Rockies, after just seven pitches, and nobody on the Rockies had put a bat on the ball yet.

Their number three hitter, Max Kalfus, did put his bat on the next pitch Andre threw, hitting it over Jerry York's head in right for a double. Then he stole third. He came home when an outside pitch that Hawk could have caught tipped off his glove and went behind him.

It was 3–0. Andre collected himself and got three ground balls after that to finally end the inning.

Hawk was talking to himself all the way to the bench. "I stink, I stink, I stink!" he said.

"Not as bad as I do," Andre said.

Coach came over and put his arms around both of them. "Now even though I think this has the potential to be a lively debate about which one of you stinks more, how about you both stop feeling sorry for yourselves so we can all have some fun coming back on these suckers?"

"Only the top of the first," Jack said. "We've got all night to do it."

The game was a mess, lots of scoring, fun to play as long as you weren't one of the guys pitching. Or if you weren't Brett Hawkins, who really did look as if he were learning to play baseball all over again.

Or maybe hadn't learned in the first place.

Andre gave way to Gregg Leonard after the second. Gregg didn't pitch a lot in relief, but his dad trusted him because he was a strike thrower. But the Rockies were hitting strikes all over the ballpark tonight. So were the Rays. By the time Jerry York somehow managed to pitch a one-two-three inning in the top of the fifth, the Rockies were ahead 12–8.

The Rays went down in order in the bottom of the inning. Jerry gave up a couple of hits in the top of the sixth, but finally stranded them on second and third. It was last ups for the Rays. The top of the order was leading off: T.W., Gregg, Jack, Gus after that if at least one guy got on.

"I haven't been in a game my team lost since last year," Jack said to Gus.

"So let's do this."

T.W. beat out a bunt. Gregg singled to right. T.W. probably shouldn't have been trying for third, down four runs, but their rightfielder couldn't throw him out. Just like that, the Rays were in business.

The Rockies' closer was Steve Stewart. He was small but had a big arm, Jack knew from when they'd played a couple of weeks ago. And he was a hard thrower who had control. He was the same as Jack, then: a kid who actually knew how to throw strikes without throwing them over the middle of the plate.

Jack had paid attention to the way he'd pitched to Gregg Leonard, trying to work him away, Gregg doing a great job of taking an outside strike to right.

Steve tried to put his first pitch to Jack low and on the outside corner. And it was on the corner, all right. It just wasn't low enough. It was up in what Gus had always called Jack's "happy zone." Jack Callahan was one of those guys who had as much power to the opposite field as he did pulling the ball, like Miguel Cabrera of the Tigers, somebody Jack thought was the best hitter in the world.

Jack was all over it, hitting the ball as hard as any ball he'd hit this season. He knew it was gone before anybody at Highland Park did.

As he ran toward first, he saw the Rockies' rightfielder turn to chase the ball. Then he saw the kid come to a dead stop, knowing he was wasting his time. The rightfielder watched the ball disappear with ease over the fence. The home run made the score 12–11.

They were still a run down. But nobody was out. Jack just gave Gus a quick high five on his way past him, not wanting to act as if he'd done anything other than make the game close.

"Keep it going," he said.

"On it," Gus said.

Gus singled to left. Andre struck out. Jerry York singled to left. Gus stopped at second. He was the tying run, Jerry was the winning run.

Hawk at the plate.

Jack knew this happened all the time in sports and was happening now: Hawk was getting the chance to win the game after having done so much to lose it for the Rays.

Steve Stewart came right at him, not trying to work the corners anymore. Hawk hit the ball on the nose. Right at their shortstop, who was moving to his left as the ball was hit. The shortstop fielded it cleanly, stepped on second, then threw to first for the double play that ended the game.

The play was close at first, but Hawk was clearly out and knew it. They all did. Hawk stood about ten feet past the base, but staring at the field ump as if hoping he might change his mind. Finally he walked slowly back to the bench, head down, batting helmet in his hand. Jack got to him first and tried to console him, telling him he'd hit the ball on the nose. Then more of the Rays were around him, telling Hawk it was just one bad game. Telling him they'd bounce back on Thursday.

But Hawk just wanted to sit at the end of their bench and be left alone.

Before Jack walked over to where his parents were waiting for him, he saw Cassie. She'd come over to watch the end of the Rays-Rockies game after having already won her own.

"You need a catcher," she said.

"I think I know one," Jack said.

TWENTY-EIGHT

N o," Teddy said. "No way."

"You can do this," Jack said.

They were in Jack's backyard the next day after school. There was no official practice scheduled for either the Rays or the Orioles.

But after Jack told Coach Leonard about Teddy, and how he thought Teddy was a good enough catcher to help him, Coach told Jack he was available to work out with Teddy on short notice.

"You know I can't promise him a spot on the team," Coach had told Jack over the phone. "I'm not sure the league will even allow us to add a player who never tried out for the league this late in the season."

"Tell all the other coaches they can tell their players that it's the kid they call Teddy Bear Madden," Jack had said. "The guys will be begging for him to join our team."

But first Jack had to persuade Teddy to try out for Coach.

"I'd rather go back to Small Falls than even think about playing for your team," Teddy said.

"We need a catcher. I told Coach you can catch better than anybody we've got."

"Forget about catching," Teddy said. "I can't play! It's why I quit playing!"

"If I didn't think you could do it, I wouldn't be talking to you."

"You're trying to win a championship," Teddy said. "And I'm . . . I'm me. You'd be better off playing Scott on his broken ankle."

They were sitting in the grass, Jack's Pedroia and Teddy's mitt between them.

"I'd do a lot for you, Jack. But not this. Uh-uh. Not happening."

"You'd be doing me a big favor if you'd at least try out."

"No, you've got it all wrong. I'm going to do you a big favor and not try out."

"What have you got to lose? Think of it that way."

"You know what I have to lose? Face. If I do this and fall on my face, I go right back to being the same joke to Gus and the guys that I always was."

He picked up his glove and stood up. "You can go ahead and cancel our workout."

"Wait," Jack said.

"I'm done talking about this," Teddy said, looking past Jack, like he was looking for the fastest way back to the house.

Jack moved slightly so he was standing in Teddy's way, looking him in the eyes. "I'm asking you as a friend."

"Please don't."

"Already did. Only you and Coach and I will know. He said he'd meet us at the field at school. He's got all of Scott's catching gear in his car. If he looks at you and decides the whole thing is a big waste of time, then it's no harm, no foul."

Teddy put his head down, then shook it slowly from side to side. "It's easy enough for me to make a fool out of myself on my own. You and Cassie and Gus saw that at the Falls. I don't need any help doing it."

"I'm the one asking for your help," Jack said. "If you say yes, I'll never ask again."

Teddy just stared back at him, his face telling Jack nothing. Then he said, "Yeah, you will. Ask for my help again. It's what friends do."

"So you'll do this?"

Teddy nodded, then grinned.

"One favor?"

"Anything," Jack said.

"Call Coach and tell him to bring Scotty's cup," he said. He grinned again and said, "And you know what kind of cup I mean."

TWENTY-NINE

When they got to the field, Teddy said he had to get something from his house before they started. When he came back, he was wearing new baseball spikes he'd never mentioned buying, and a red Cardinals cap.

"Cardinals?" Jack said.

"I watched a few games and like that Molina guy who catches for them."

"You like catchers now, huh?"

"Shut up."

"You sound like Cassie."

"You'd be better off putting her on the team," Teddy said.

Coach showed up fifteen minutes later. He said to Teddy, "I hear Callahan has turned you into a ballplayer."

"He thinks he has."

"It's all in the coaching," Jack said.

"See there," Coach said, "that's what I'm always trying to tell you and your teammates!" In a quieter voice he said to Teddy, "Are you sure you want to do this, son?"

"I do," Teddy said, then looked over at Jack and said, "No joke."

Coach pitched to Teddy first, throwing balls high and then in the dirt and then inside and outside, a lot more outside, wanting to see if Teddy could reach across his body and make backhand catches. Jack stood out near second and watched them, understanding as he did what it must be like to be Coach Leonard or any of the other coaches in the league, rooting for the kids on their team to do well.

After about twenty pitches, Coach said he was going to change it up. He told Teddy that when he called out "Stealing!" he wanted him to come up throwing to Jack at second.

The first time, Teddy threw the ball high and wide over Jack.

He was trying to put too much on the ball. The second time he did the same.

The third one, though, was perfect, right on the bag. Jack pretended that he was putting a tag on an imaginary runner. He saw Teddy smiling at him from the plate, mask in hand. He gave a small nod to Jack. Jack nodded back.

About five minutes later, Teddy made another great throw, but Coach said, "Don't move too early, even though there's no batter. In a real game, if the guy had been swinging, he would've clipped you in the head."

"Sorry," Teddy said.

"Don't apologize," Coach said, talking to him like he was a real player already.

"Just don't do it again," Coach Leonard said.

Teddy didn't. Before long Coach had moved Jack over to stand on first. Then he'd call out "Bunt!" every few pitches and roll the ball either toward the first-base side of the field or the third-base side. Teddy would come out of the box—maybe surprising Coach with his quickness—pounce on the ball, pick it up with his bare hand, and gun it to Jack.

They took a break for some Gatorade. When they were ready to go, Coach asked Teddy if he was ready to hit. Teddy said he was. Coach asked if he had his own bat, and Teddy said he didn't but that he was going to use Jack's Easton. When Coach went back to his car for his bag of old practice balls, Jack said to Teddy, "You're doing awesome."

"Let's not get crazy here."

"Don't try to kill the ball. Just meet it."

"Who's the coach here, you or Mr. Leonard?"

"Both."

Teddy went over to the bench and took off his shin guards and chest protector. Jack sat next to him.

"Even if Coach wants me," Teddy said, "you really think the guys on the team will?"

"They want to win," Jack said.

When Coach came back with the balls, he told Jack to get out on the mound and pitch to Teddy.

"Do not go easy on me," Teddy said. "I mean it."

"I won't."

Teddy was nervous at first, even more nervous than he'd been behind the plate. He missed the first few balls badly, swinging whether they were strikes or not. And overswinging. Jack wasn't throwing his hardest; he never did that at practice. But he wasn't babying the ball either.

Finally Teddy hit a hard grounder to the left side of the infield. Then a clean single to right. Then he got quick and overanxious again, dropping his right shoulder, popping up a couple of very hittable pitches.

Coach stopped them then. He pointed to Jack and said, "Your personal coach here ever tell you to wait on the ball?"

"All the time."

"So wait on the ball."

Jack knew there were times in baseball, a lot of times, when that was easier said than done. So Teddy swung through a couple more pitches. Fouled a couple back.

Finally, though, he waited. Kept his hands back and his weight back and his head on the ball and drilled a pretty decent Jack Callahan fastball to the bottom of the rightfield wall.

Jack didn't say anything, just turned and grabbed another ball out of the bag. As he did, he smiled at Coach, who was standing on second base.

Coach smiled back.

Then he yelled in to Teddy, "Next time you hit one like that, run it out."

Three pitches later he jumped on a ball on the inside half of the plate, lined it over third base, and took off for first.

The chance to make the Rays hadn't suddenly turned him into a sprinter. He really wasn't all that much faster than he'd been the first time Jack had worked him out.

But as Jack watched him make the turn at first and head for second, watched Teddy Madden moving as well as he'd ever seen him, he thought, *If you didn't know, you'd just think he was running like a catcher.*

A real one.

When he got to second, Coach held him up and then high-fived him.

"We're done here," he said.

Jack walked out to them. He and Teddy waited until Coach Leonard said, "I have absolutely no idea what our board members are going to say about this crazy idea of ours. But if they say it's all right, you can play for me anytime, kid."

Now he put out his hand for Teddy to shake it.

The three of them scattered to go pick up balls. When they finished with that, Teddy said he had to go. He and his mom were going to Lewisboro to have dinner with his aunt.

"You did good," Coach said.

"Thanks, Coach."

"If I hear something tonight, I'll call you, or Jack will."

Teddy ran for his house as hard as he'd just run the bases.

"Interesting kid," Coach said to Jack.

As they walked to the parking lot, Jack told him just how interesting he thought Teddy was, starting with the day they'd first started to become friends at gym class, all the way to Teddy freezing at the bridge.

THE ONLY GAME

"It would be good for us if they let him play, Coach," Jack said. "But it would be great for him."

Coach told him to keep his phone on.

Two hours later he called and said, "Call your buddy and tell him he made the team."

"Yes!" Jack shouted into the phone.

"The board members I talked to seemed to understand that we weren't trying to put one over on them," Coach said. "And I explained this might be the best thing that ever happened to this boy."

"Cool," Jack said.

"You understand," Coach said, "that playing in games, especially the kind of big games we've got coming up, will be a lot more challenging than playing on an empty field with the two of us. You do understand that, right?"

Jack said he did.

But when he hung up with Coach, right before he called Teddy, he thought, *We'll cross that bridge when we come to it.*

THIRTY

With three games left in the regular season, the Rays were tied with the Rockies for the last play-off spot in the Atlantic, but still just two games out of first.

The Rays would play the Red Sox first, then the two teams ahead of them: the Rangers and the first-place White Sox. The play-offs started in ten days, if the Rays made it.

Teddy's first game was on Saturday morning. On Friday night Jack was back coaching first for the Orioles in the six o'clock game. The Orioles were still undefeated, still rolling through their league, and were expected to keep rolling tonight, because Cassie was starting. After the game, her dad was going to drop her and Jack and Teddy at Baskin-Robbins. Gus couldn't go; his grandparents were in town.

Jack still liked helping out with the Orioles, but they hadn't needed much help. And even if he wasn't still Mr. Bennett's first-base coach, he would have wanted to be at this game. He hated to miss a game when Cassie was pitching. She really was that good.

And tonight, against the Astros, she struck out the first six batters she faced. It only made the game more exciting, because by now Jack knew this girl well. She wanted to strike out nine batters in a row the way Jack had. It was still killing her that he'd done it this season and she hadn't.

"I am doing this," she said to him after the bottom of the second, and both of them knew exactly what she was talking about.

Jack grinned. "Now I don't want you overthrowing," he said. "Putting too much pressure on the old arm."

"You don't want me to do it, do you?" she said. "You want to hold that over me?"

"Wait a second," he said. "You're the one always bringing it up. I never bring it up."

She waggled a finger at him. "Oh, I know you," she said. "You feeling superior is more of an unspoken thing."

It made him laugh. "As opposed to you feeling superior being much more of a spoken thing?"

"Shut up."

The Orioles scored five runs in the top of the third, making the score 8–0 for them. Mr. Bennett told Cassie this was her last inning. They were getting ready for the play-offs too. She went back out and struck out the first two batters in the third.

The last batter before her and her own perfect night was the Astros' second baseman, a friend of hers from school named Mary Anne Mason. She was short, which meant a small strike zone. Jack remembered her being a tough out the first two times the teams had played.

Jack watched Cassie, struck as always by how fierce her concentration was, more now than ever. He knew how much she wanted this.

Her first two pitches to Mary Anne were called balls, even though Jack thought they both could have been strikes. Cassie's body language told him she felt the same way.

She came back, though, and got the count to 2–2, Mary Anne swinging and missing, and then fouling a ball off.

Cassie clearly put something extra on the next pitch, not wanting the count to go full, wanting to strike out Mary Anne right here.

The pitch was clearly outside.

Three and two.

Jack understood that in an 8–0 game, this was a big moment that existed only in Cassie's mind. He would have treated it the same way. And he was surprised at how much he wanted this for her. Maybe it was because she wanted it so much.

She went into her motion, brought her arm up and around, whipped into her underhand motion, and threw the fastest pitch she'd thrown all night, maybe all season.

Mary Anne, to her credit, knowing everybody else on her team had struck out tonight, wasn't looking for a walk. She swung at the pitch, right down the middle of the plate.

And got just enough of a piece of it to roll the ball weakly back to Cassie.

It was probably the only time that an easy out like this would make Cassie Bennett as angry as this one clearly did. She was on the ball quickly and threw it so hard to Katie Cummings at first that Jack was afraid she might knock the glove right off Katie's hand. But she didn't. Inning over, Cassie's night on the mound over.

When she came off the field, she went straight for Jack.

"Those first two pitches were strikes!" she said, keeping her voice down.

"I know."

"Well, I hope you're happy."

"I'm not," he said. "I wanted a strikeout as much as you did."

Then, out of nowhere, Cassie smiled.

"I know you did," she said.

The Orioles finally ending up winning the game, 11–3. An hour later Jack, Cassie, and Teddy were at a window table at Baskin-Robbins. By then Cassie had gone from being star pitcher to cheerleader, trying to pump Teddy up for his first game and make him less anxious about it at the same time.

"I know what you're doing," Teddy said. "I know what both of you are doing. But neither one of you has ever seen me in a real game. It's not like I quit playing baseball in the first place because I was doing so good."

"Doesn't matter," Cassie said. "You're a different guy now." She pointed her spoon at Jack. "He knows it. I know it. Red Sox are gonna find out tomorrow."

"I keep telling you this," Jack said. "If Coach didn't think you could play, you wouldn't be on the team."

He tried to reach over with his spoon and get some of Cassie's Pralines 'n Cream, thinking she wasn't paying attention, but she blocked him with her hand.

"I told you," she said. "I don't share."

"I thought you were just kidding."

"I wasn't." She grinned and moved her bowl slightly closer to herself and focused on Teddy again.

"What's the thing that scares you the most?"

"That I have a chance to screw up the team's whole season and keep them from punching their way into the tournament for the World Series. Other than that, nothing much."

"That's nuts," Jack said. "If we end up missing the play-offs by one game, it's going to be my fault, not yours, for missing the first four games."

Cassie whistled. It was one more thing she was really, really good at. "Wow," she said. "This is the first pity party I've ever been to with ice cream, even though nothing you two are worried about has happened yet. Or is going to happen."

"Just trust yourself the way I trust you," Jack said.

"You're just saying that because you have to."

"Because I want to."

Cassie said, "Jack has many shortcomings, just because he's a guy. But he never lies."

They pooled their money and paid the check and walked outside. On both sides of the street you could see kids still in their baseball uniforms, walking in packs of five or six or with their parents. Friday night in Walton. Baseball town.

Jack heard a bark of laughter from across the street, in front of Cold Stone, and saw a group of high school boys, a couple of whom he recognized.

For a moment, just a moment, Jack imagined Brad standing there with them.

He slapped Teddy on the back and said, "It's gonna be great tomorrow."

Teddy said, "I did sign up for this, didn't I?"

Jack nodded and smiled, because he was hearing his brother's voice inside his head.

"You did," he said to Teddy Madden. "Now you gotta wear it."

THIRTY-ONE

Teddy's mom dropped him off at Jack's house a couple of hours before the Rays' game against the Red Sox. Jack had told Teddy they were going to have their own pregame workout before the real one at Highland Park.

When Jack opened the front door, what he saw made him smile.

Teddy had his own bat bag now. Without saying anything, he pulled out the same kind of Easton bat that Jack owned.

His was just in different colors, orange and black.

"You dog!" Jack said.

"I just hope I don't play like one."

"You won't."

"I feel like it's the first day of school," Teddy said.

Jack pointed a finger at him. "Hey!" he said. "Do not compare baseball to school ever again."

It got a quick smile out of Teddy, as nervous as he was acting.

"C'mon," Jack said, leading him out to the backyard. "Let's throw."

As they warmed up, Jack reminded Teddy that the worst thing for a catcher—or anyone on the field, really—was to start throwing the ball around when there was no chance to get an out.

"Wasted throws become errors, and errors become cheap runs," Jack said. "If you can see you have no shot at a guy stealing today, or trying to take an extra base, hold the ball."

"Got it."

"But if you do have a chance, trust it. Your arm is as good as Scott's."

Teddy said, "You're sure he can't play on a broken ankle?"

"This is gonna be great, you'll see," Jack said. "There's nothing better than a big game."

"I was pretty happy watching games from up in the stands."

"It's way better when you're down on the field," Jack said. "You helped me get back out there. Now I'm just doing the same for you."

Jack saw his dad on the back porch, pointing at his watch. It was time to go. The two of them walked across the yard in their uniforms. Teddy looked down at the team name, written in white script across the pale blue jersey.

"I still can't believe I'm with the Rays," Teddy said.

"It's even better than that," Jack said. "You're with me."

"Because you're my friend?"

"Well, yeah," Jack said. "But mostly because I'm your starting pitcher."

The other guys on the team were great with Teddy. From the time he'd shown up, they'd treated him like he'd been with them from the start.

Brett Hawkins was the first to come over and high-five Teddy.

"You couldn't show up a game sooner so I didn't look like a *Bad News Bears* reject?" Hawk said.

Gus said, "Just be glad he's here now. Because our next option at catcher was going to be even more pathetic—me."

"Whoa," Hawk said. "You're saying that you're a worse catcher than I am? No way."

Teddy sat down at the end of the bench and strapped on his shin guards for infield practice. Gregg Leonard sat on one side of him, Jerry York on the other.

Jerry pointed at the shin guards and said, "You know which side of those bad boys is supposed to be on the front of your leg, right?"

"I better," Teddy said, "once Jack starts short-hopping fastballs to me."

"Listen to the chirp from the new guy," Jerry said. "He sounds ready to me."

"Don't worry," Jack said. "He is."

He hoped.

Teddy seemed to relax a little during infield practice, standing next to Coach Leonard while the coach hit ground balls, even to Jack on the pitcher's mound. Every few minutes Coach would tell Teddy to step out in front of the plate and throw to one of the bases. Most of the throws, Jack saw, were strong and accurate.

When they came off the field, ready to start batting practice, Jack patted Teddy on the back. "You looked good out there," he said.

"Let's see what happens when there's guys on the bases trying to make me look bad."

It was when he got into the batter's box with his brand-new

bat that he looked nervous, producing a series of swings and misses, weak pop-ups, and even weaker ground balls. From the mound Coach told him to stay in there and take some extra swings. Teddy finally hit a clean single to center, and Coach told him to quit on that one.

When they were all back at the bench, Coach put his arm around Teddy and said, "You just concentrate on defense tonight, okay? Anything you give me on offense in your first game will be gravy."

"Coach," Teddy said, grinning at him, "can we please not talk about gravy?"

Coach laughed. So did Jack. As nervous as Teddy was, he was still Teddy.

They were just a few minutes from the top of the first, the Rays batting first today. Jack saw Cassie leaning over the fence behind the Rays' bench, waving him and Teddy over.

"Just remember," she said to Teddy when they got to her. "If you look good tonight, it will make me look great."

Teddy said, "How do you figure?"

"Are you kidding?" she said. "You're asking me that after all the instruction I've given you?"

"I thought Teddy and I did most of the work," Jack said.

"Well, that's your version," Cassie said. "I have my own."

"Shocker," Jack said.

"Let's do this for Cassie," she said, putting up her right hand for a high five from Teddy.

"Let's do this, period," Teddy said.

Jack grinned at Cassie and said, "Can you believe how competitive this guy is?"

As they walked back to the field, Jack said, "We're just going out there and playing catch."

"Is the whole game going to be one long pep talk?" Teddy said.

"Pretty much."

Jack turned and looked into the stands. Today Teddy's mom was in Brad's old spot next to Jack's mom. Instinctively Jack reached back and felt Brad's note, his good luck charm, in his pocket where it always was.

Big bro, he thought, *today we're going to need enough luck for two.*

The Rays scored twice in the top of the first. Jack tripled home Gregg with one out, then Gus singled home Jack. Gus ended up being stranded at third. Teddy, batting ninth, would have to wait for his first at bat of the season.

Teddy was already behind the plate when Jack got to the mound. Jack took his warm-up tosses, and Teddy threw down to second. No more pep talks now. Teddy was officially on the field and in the game. It was time to play. Jack was determined to get Teddy through the early innings, no matter what. He wanted to make things as easy for him as he possibly could.

The problem was that Teddy made things hard on himself. The Red Sox leadoff hitter, Zack Claiborne, swung and missed at an 0–2 pitch. But Teddy either took his eye off the ball or just flat missed it. The ball tipped off his mitt and skipped behind him to the screen. Zack made it down to first easily.

Even with Jack pitching from the stretch, Zack got a great jump on him and stole second on the first pitch. Teddy had no chance to throw him out and wisely held the ball.

The Red Sox were clearly going to test the new guy right away. So Zack took off for third on the next pitch. Teddy made a solid throw down there, but T.W.—starting the game at third in place of Hawk, who was taking Jack's spot at short—dropped the ball.

Jack called time and waved Teddy out to the mound.

"Sorry," Teddy said.

Jack grinned. "Shut up," he said. "The guy's not scoring. I'm gonna strike out the side, and no matter what, you're gonna catch the ball and keep it in front of you."

"Sounds like a plan."

Jack did strike out the next two guys. He went to a full count on the Red Sox cleanup hitter, Andy Gundling. Jack threw him a screaming fastball, one that should have been a called strike three.

But Teddy missed this one too.

A lot happened next.

Teddy went for the ball, which was rolling a few feet away from him, toward first. Zack dashed for the plate from third base. Jack ran for the plate himself but could see that he was going to be late if Teddy tried to toss him the ball.

Somehow, though, Teddy Madden was thinking like a ballplayer. Like a catcher. When he picked up the ball, he gave a quick glance at Zack and saw he had no chance to even dive at home plate and make a tag on him. Instead he turned back toward first base, threw a perfect strike to Gus, and got Andy Gundling by a stride for the third out of the inning.

When Teddy saw the field ump's hand go up, signaling the out, Teddy made the same gesture himself. Then he took off his mask and looked at Jack and nodded. Neither one of them said a word, and neither one had to.

Now Teddy was really in the game.

THIRTY-TWO

t was still 2–0, Rays, when Henry Koepp replaced Jack on the mound in the bottom of the fourth. Teddy had struck out his first time up, swinging at a pitch that was nearly over his head. And he'd made a throwing error in the bottom of the third, throwing the ball over Hawk's head when Zack tried to steal second. Zack took third on the play but stayed there when Jack got the next batter to ground to Gus at first.

So far, so good, Jack thought. Teddy was making normal mistakes, but none of them had cost the Rays yet.

Until the fourth.

Andy Gundling led off for the Red Sox with a home run that just cleared the leftfield fence. Kevin Malone, their catcher, singled after that. He wasn't a fast runner, but he took off for second. Jack was at second in plenty of time to take the throw. He thought Teddy had more than enough time to throw Kevin out. Only this time Teddy held the ball when he should have thrown it. Kevin took off for third two pitches later. Teddy bounced his throw to Hawk, who made a terrific play, keeping the ball in front of them and Kevin at third.

Their next hitter hit a short fly ball to center field. Gregg Leonard came running in for the ball and caught it in stride as Kevin tagged up at third. Gregg wasn't just their best outfielder, he had the best arm in the outfield, and he showed it off now, making a perfect one-hop throw home.

It couldn't have been a better throw for Teddy to handle if Gregg had run all the way in from center and handed it to him. Only Teddy took his eye off it to see where Kevin was. He looked like he was trying to tag him out before the ball actually got to him. The ball bounced off his chest protector, Kevin scored, and the game was tied at 2–2.

Henry held them there. After the third out, Teddy came

off the field, head down, as if the Red Sox had won the game instead of just tied it with two more innings to play.

He went over to Gregg and said, "I managed to turn a perfect throw into a run for them."

The coach's son said, "We don't apologize on this team. We just figure out a way to get the run back. Okay?"

He wasn't joking, and Teddy knew it from the tone of his voice.

"Okay," Teddy said.

There were two runners on for the Rays, second and third, when Teddy came up in the top of the fifth with two out. But he tried too hard to get a hit and struck out on three pitches. The game was still tied.

In the bottom of the fifth, it was Zack Claiborne torturing them on the bases again. He got a two-out single off Jerry York and stole second easily. When Teddy sailed a throw over Hawk as he tried to steal third, Zack jogged home with the run that gave the Red Sox the lead.

Teddy started to say something to Jack when the Rays were getting ready to hit in the top of the sixth. It was their last ups if they couldn't make something happen, but Jack stopped him.

"Game's not over," he said.

Gus came over and pounded Jack some fist, then Teddy.

"You know what we call this?" he said. "Winning time."

Jack was leading off for the Rays. He hit the second pitch he saw from the Red Sox closer, Jay Hill, over the rightfield wall, crushing it. The game was tied again. Then Gus Morales hit the first pitch he saw from Jay over the leftfield wall, back-to-back homers for the first time all season.

Now the Rays were ahead by a run, 4–3. Jay got three straight outs after that. Now Jerry York had the chance to close out the game in the bottom of the sixth.

Jack sat next to Teddy as he put on his chest protector. In a quiet voice Teddy said, "You ever get scared?"

"All the time," Jack said.

"How do you get over it?"

"You don't," Jack said. "You just tell yourself that this is why you play."

Somehow Teddy managed a smile behind his catcher's mask. "Oh good," he said. "'Cause I was starting to wonder."

The game ended this way:

The Red Sox with runners on second and third, two outs. Tying run at third, winning run at second. A base hit would win for them. An out would win for the Rays. The Red Sox centerfielder, Adam Weiss, at the plate, the count two balls and two strikes.

Jerry threw him the kind of pitch that pitchers called filthy, an inside fastball, at the knees, hard to hit, too close to take in a moment where a called third strike ended the game.

But Adam put a good swing on the ball, too good, muscling

the ball deep into the shortstop hole. Maybe when it came off the bat it looked like a single to left that was going to split Jack and Hawk, and a game-winning RBI.

Just not to Jack.

He read the ball perfectly off the bat and got a tremendous jump on it, doing what he'd always done and gliding to the ball. Jack backhanded the ball on the outfield grass. As he did, he could see Andy Gundling, the runner on third, stumble slightly as he broke for home.

Jack knew how fast Adam was and how long the throw was to first. His only chance for an out was to plant as well as he could, even with his momentum taking him into short left-field, and throw home.

To Teddy.

He had the plate blocked the way Jack had taught him. He reached for the ball as Andy went into his slide.

Jack watched the play from his knees, at the edge of the infield grass:

Catcher. Ball. Runner.

Everything happening at once.

Jack wondering if Teddy could hold on to the throw this time.

At winning time.

He held on to the throw.

When the dust cleared, there was Teddy showing the

home-plate ump that the ball was still in the pocket of his mitt. The ump took one last look down and saw that Andy's foot still hadn't touched home plate, because Teddy had blocked it like a champ with his shin guard.

The ump pointed at the plate then, jerked his right arm up in the air, and yelled, "You're out, son."

Rays 4, Red Sox 3.

Final.

THIRTY-THREE

Jack and Teddy and Gus and Cassie were in Jack's backyard later in the afternoon, having just finished a game of Wiffle ball Home Run Derby.

It was Jack and Teddy against the team of Gus and Cassie. Gus and Cassie's team won on their last swing, Cassie hitting a pitch from Jack over the hedges at the end of the yard and acting as if she'd just hit a walk-off to win the championship of the entire planet.

She followed it by running a victory lap around the yard, full of whoops and fist pumps.

"Girls rule," she yelled. "Boys drool."

"Wait a second," Gus said. "Weren't we on the same team?"

"You know I carried you," she said.

When she finished her lap, Jack said, "You do know what a truly awful winner you are, right?"

"Only with you guys," she said. "Never with my girls."

Teddy said, "Are we supposed to thank you for that?"

They all went and sat in the shade of the big old willow tree, drinking the lemonade Jack's mom had just brought out to them and eating chocolate chip cookies.

"I hit the game-winning homer, Mrs. Callahan," Cassie said.

"I heard," Jack's mom said.

"So did people in Florida," Jack said.

"He's just jealous," his mom said to Cassie, then reached down and high-fived her. "Girls rule," she said.

Then they were replaying the big game, again. They talked about Jack's home run and Teddy knowing enough to ignore the runner trying to score and throwing to first. Of course they talked about the play that had won it for the Rays. As always, you didn't need a video to see the big plays and the big moments in the game you'd just played. They were burned into your memory, and maybe your imagination.

"You guys bailed me out," Teddy said.

"You bailed us out by making that tag!" Gus said.

"You can keep talking about how you have to get better," Cassie said to Teddy. "And you're going to get better. But you still made the play you had to make. So shut up about the ones you didn't make."

She punctuated the thought by leaning over and pinching his arm.

"That hurt!" Teddy said.

"It was supposed to," Cassie said.

"You know the games are only gonna get bigger for these guys, right?" Teddy said to Cassie, pointing at Jack and Gus.

"For us," Jack said. "You're one of us now."

Cassie pinched Teddy again. "So get with the program, big boy."

They ate and drank in silence for a couple of minutes until Cassie said to Teddy, "Tell the truth—what were you thinking about when the ball and the runner and the whole game were coming right at you?"

"You want the truth?"

Cassie nodded.

"I was thinking about the last thing Jack told me before the game started," Teddy said. "That we were just going to have a game of catch. So I told myself to catch the ball."

"But you blocked the plate, too," Gus said.

"Hey," Teddy said, "that was the easy part. I'm a lot bigger than Andy. He probably thought he was trying to slide through . . . what?" He looked at them. "Little help here."

Jack smiled and said, "A bear?"

Teddy smiled back at him.

"Yeah," he said. "A big, bad bear."

Teddy stayed a few minutes longer after Gus and Cassie left. Before he got on his bike to leave, Jack said, "One last question: How did it feel?"

Teddy said, "It felt great."

Then he said, "For that one minute, I knew what it's like to be you."

"Nah," Jack said. "That was all you, dude."

Teddy got on his bike and rode away. Jack watched him until he disappeared around the corner.

Yeah, he thought, *a whole new Teddy Bear Madden.*

This one was the catcher for the Rays.

The Rays won again on Tuesday night against the Rangers. Andre pitched his best game of the season, and everybody in the batting order got a hit, including Teddy in his last at bat, a bloop single to right over the second baseman's head.

Teddy was still making rookie mistakes behind the plate. He still wasn't trusting his arm the way Jack thought he should be.

But it didn't matter on a night when the final score was 11–4, and the Rays were in second place in the Atlantic by themselves.

Even better, the Rockies had beaten the White Sox in their last at bat. So this Saturday's game against the White Sox would be for the top seed in the play-offs. Jack knew it was more for pride than anything else, pride and last ups in the title game if it came to that.

But it was a lot of pride on the line for all of them. After everything that had happened, the way the season had started for Jack and for his team, they had put themselves in a position where if they just kept winning, they'd win the championship of the Atlantic and play themselves into the County All-Star League.

If they won that, they had played themselves into the tournament for the Little League World Series. That was just a dream at the start of the season. Now it was in reach.

It was Jack starting against Nate Vinton in the last game of the regular season. The Rays' best against their best. Coach Leonard had decided to start Jack against the Sox. Andre would start in their first play-off game next Wednesday, then Jack again in the finals on Saturday night if they made it that far.

"I can't start you twice in the play-offs, anyway," said Coach Leonard, "not with just one day's rest. So you go today, and then you've got all the rest you need for the big game. We're gonna play this one today like the play-offs are starting right now."

"Stay on a roll," Jack said.

"All the way through next Saturday night."

Coach didn't think they were going to lose any more games this season, and neither did Jack.

"Sounds right," he said to Coach.

"Right as rain."

It was one of his favorite expressions.

"Coach," Jack said, "I've always wanted to ask you: What does that mean, right as rain?"

Coach shrugged and blew a huge bubble with his gum. "No clue," he said.

The stands were full on both sides of the field. The Rays, as home team, had the first-base side. The top row was Jack's parents, Mrs. Madden, and Gus's parents. Cassie had told Jack not to look for her in the stands; she was going to wander.

"I can't stay in one spot. I get too nervous," she'd said to Jack.

"More nervous than when your own team is playing?"

The Orioles, still unbeaten, would play for the championship of their league on Monday night.

"Way more nervous," she said. "With you guys, I'm not in control."

"Never a good thing for you."

"Torture." He knew she was telling the truth. When the Rangers game was still close, right before the Rays blew it open with seven runs in the fourth, he'd looked down the rightfield line at one point and seen her peeking at the action from behind a tree.

Right before the Rays took the field, Jack said to Teddy, "How you feeling?"

"Other than the fact that I'm having trouble breathing, feeling just great."

"I've always felt that breathing in baseball was totally overrated."

"Can I ask you one favor?"

"Anything."

"Can we have it not come down to the last play today?"

"I'll do my best," Jack said. "If you promise to remember one thing."

"To start breathing eventually?"

"To remember that even though I always say this is the only game, it's still a game."

"Even today?"

"Especially today."

Jack had a case of nerves himself. But he kept telling himself they were good nerves. He knew that the season wasn't on the line against the White Sox. They were in the play-offs win or lose. But in sports, first place was still first place. Coach Leonard had another expression that covered that one: "If you're not the lead dog, the view is always the same."

Jack wanted the Rays to be the lead dogs today. Then he proceeded to go out and pitch the sloppiest inning he'd had in weeks.

THIRTY-
FOUR

He walked their leadoff man, Wayne Coffey, even though he hated walking the first batter of an inning, and especially the first inning. When Teddy threw the ball back to him, Jack snatched it out of the air in disgust.

He followed that by doing the worst thing you could do as a pitcher: He was still thinking about the last batter instead of focusing on the next one. He was still mad at himself and tried to overthrow his first pitch to Conor Freeman, the White Sox shortstop, and threw it so far behind him that it hit him in the butt.

"Sorry!" Jack said to Conor, walking toward home plate. "You okay?"

Conor waved him off, grinning at him. They'd been playing ball with and against each other since they were six years old.

"Not hurt," he said. "Just shocked."

"Me too," Jack said.

First and second, nobody out. His next pitch, to Nate Vinton, was a ball in the dirt that handcuffed Teddy completely, a wild pitch that ended up behind him. Now the Sox had second and third, nobody out. Nate then laced the 1–0 pitch over Gregg Leonard's head for a triple. It was 2–0, White Sox, and Jack hadn't thrown a strike yet.

He threw one to Mike O'Keeffe, actually got ahead of him 0–2, but Mike managed to hit a sacrifice fly to right and it was 3–0. Jack struck out the next two batters to get out of the inning, but the damage had been done. He had put his team into an early hole.

"I pitched better my first game back," he said to Gus on the bench.

"Can I tell you something you're always telling me without you biting my head off?"

"Go ahead."

"Get over it," Gus said. "They're not going to let you pitch the first inning all over again, so I'm pretty sure you can't do anything about what just happened. So get over it."

He did, not allowing the Sox another run before he went out to play shortstop in the top of the fourth. But the score was still 3–0, because Nate was the one dealing today. He was showing off an even better fastball than the last time they'd played, and with even better control of it. After he struck out Teddy to end the top of the third, it was nine up and nine down for the Rays. Nate had five strikeouts.

"He's pitching the way I was supposed to," Jack said to Gus and Teddy on the bench. The top of the order was getting ready to hit against Nate in the top of the fourth.

Nate was finishing his warm-up pitches, his dad having allowed him to pitch one more inning.

"I'm glad he's still out there," Gus said.

"Why?" Teddy said.

"Because we've still got a chance to ruin his day."

The Rays did their best. T.W. Stanley singled, for their first hit and their first base runner. Gregg Leonard walked. Jack whistled a single right past Nate's ear, making him duck out of the way, and the Rays were on the board. Gus followed with a double and just like that, it was 3–2. They were in business.

"New game," Gus said when they headed back onto the field.

Jack said, "I like this one much better."

Henry Koepp came in for the Rays, trying to keep it a one-run game.

Only Teddy picked this inning to act as if he really was playing his first game all over again.

He dropped a third strike, couldn't find the ball behind him, and allowed Conor to reach first. Then Nate, their best hitter, surprised everybody by laying down a perfect bunt up the first-base line. Teddy, as surprised as anybody, was slow getting to the ball and should have seen he had no chance to get Nate at first.

He tried anyway and put too much on his throw. The ball sailed over Gus's head, and suddenly a bunt that had rolled about twenty feet up the line was on its way to becoming an inside-the-park home run. By the time Jerry York chased down the ball in the rightfield corner, Nate was the one chasing Conor Freeman home, and the White Sox were ahead 5–2.

Henry walked Mike O'Keeffe. When Mike took off for second, Teddy tried to aim the ball instead of cutting it loose, obviously afraid to throw another ball into the outfield. The ball dove into the dirt about six feet in front of Jack, and he had no chance to get a glove on it as it took a crazy hop past him. When he picked it up in short center, Mike was on third.

The next White Sox batter hit a ground ball right at Jack, who'd moved in to the infield grass, because Coach wanted them to at least get a chance to cut down the run if somebody did hit the ball on the ground. Jack gloved the ball cleanly and threw a perfect strike to Teddy, thinking as the ball was in the air that it might have been the best pitch he'd thrown all night.

With Mike bearing down on him, Teddy dropped the ball. Now the White Sox were ahead 6–2. Even then, the Rays didn't quit. Jack doubled with one out in the sixth, Gus doubled him home. It was 6–3. Hawk struck out for the second out. But Henry walked and so did Jerry York. Still a chance. Andre hit a little RBI roller that died between home and third and the bases were still loaded.

For Teddy.

Somehow the game had found Teddy in its biggest moment.

If Teddy could keep the inning going, they were back to the top of the order one last time, and anything could happen after that.

What actually happened: Teddy Madden struck out on three pitches, and they weren't going to finish in first place after all.

When they'd finished shaking hands with the White Sox, Jack looked around for Teddy.

But he'd already gone home.

Teddy didn't return any of Jack's calls or texts for the rest of Saturday afternoon and into Saturday night. So Jack was surprised when he did get a text from him Sunday morning.

Jack:

YEAH, MAN, WHEN AND WHERE?

Teddy:

SCHOOL NOW.

Teddy was waiting for him in the dugout. On his way across the field, Jack was thinking that a lot had happened in that dugout in just one season, for him and for Teddy.

When Jack sat down on the steps across from Teddy, he said, "I don't think you've ever been the one who wanted to work out."

"I never needed it as much as I do today."

"Fine with me," Jack said. "A day without baseball is never as good as one with it."

Scott Sutter's catcher's mitt, the one Teddy was still using because it was broken in perfectly, was next to him on the bench. His blue Rays cap was on top of the mitt. But Teddy wasn't ready to work out just yet. Jack could see something was on his mind.

"You okay?" Jack said.

Teddy shook his head. "Nope."

"Listen," Jack said. "I know we lost yesterday, but it's not the end of the world. Even if we'd won, we'd still have to win two more games to win the championship."

Teddy said, "No pep talks today, okay?"

"That wasn't a pep talk," Jack said, and shrugged. "It is what it is."

Teddy took a deep breath, blew it out. "I can't do this," he said.

"Why?" Jack said. "Because of yesterday? How about the way I pitched? It's a good thing it wasn't one and done like the play-offs. If it was, we'd be done like dinner."

"Maybe next year I'll be ready for games like this," Teddy said. "But I'm not ready for them right now. I'm gonna end up screwing this thing up for you guys."

"It's not 'you guys' anymore. It's us. You're one of us now, which means we're all in this together."

"I know that sounds great," Teddy said. "I do." He shook his head. "But I did more to help the other team than ours."

"You're our catcher."

"The worst one on any team in the play-offs."

"Dude," Jack said. "You gotta stop talking like this. And thinking like this. Because I'm telling you, you are ready for this."

"I'm not." Jack started to say something, and Teddy put out a hand to stop him. "I worry all the time about making mistakes. I wake up in the night sometimes and I've been dreaming about making mistakes. And then when I do make one on the field, I press more and make two others. I'm scared all the time."

He looked up at Jack with big eyes and said, "I feel like I'm back at the bridge."

"C'mon, that's totally different."

"No," Teddy said. "It's not."

"It'll get easier," Jack said. "It's like my dad is always telling me, it's just reps."

"I keep trying to tell you, but you won't listen: I'm not you!"

"Nobody's asking you to be. Just be yourself."

"I am being myself," Teddy said. "Scared."

"Everybody gets scared. It's a part of sports, finding a way to get past it. I can help you do that."

"But you can't make the catches for me or the throws or hit for me," Teddy said. He shrugged. "I wish sometimes I could get some kind of injury and have a good reason to quit."

"You're not quitting."

"I know." Teddy shrugged again. "I wish I had something funny to say, but I don't. So let's play."

They soft-tossed for a few minutes. Then Jack had Teddy

do some drills where Jack purposely threw balls in the dirt, showing him all over again how easy it was to slide and get his body in front of the ball and keep it in front of him. Before they finished, Jack went out to second and put his glove out when Teddy would come up throwing, as if he were the catcher giving a target to the pitcher.

When they were done, Jack said, "I know you don't want to hear this today. But I watch you now and can't believe what you looked like when we started."

"You're a good teacher," Teddy said. "I just gotta become a better pupil this week."

"You did this, not me. And you know why? Because you secretly love it."

Teddy couldn't help himself. He smiled. "You don't give up, do you?"

"And if you think I ever will, you don't know me nearly as well as you think you do."

"I give up," Teddy said. "Check you later."

Teddy watched him walk slowly in the direction of his house, Scott's mitt in his hand, his Rays cap turned backward on his head, his head down.

Jack knew Teddy believed everything he'd told him, knew that when Teddy got out of his own way, he was a good catcher and a good ballplayer. And nobody knew better than Jack how you could build things up in your own mind and make them much worse than they really were. Doing that had nearly cost him his season, the season that was ending now with Teddy as his teammate and his friend.

Jack watched Teddy until he climbed the short fence in the distance. He'd never looked back, like he was lost in his own world.

When Teddy was finally out of sight, Jack thought, *Now I'm the one who's scared.*

THIRTY-FIVE

Jack and Teddy and Gus watched somebody else play for the title the next night.

Jack did it from the Orioles' bench, and from the first-base coach's box. Teddy and Gus did it from the stands on the first-base side of the front field at Highland Park.

They all watched Cassie and her team try to beat the Dodgers and finish off an unbeaten season.

The Dodgers had lost only two games during the regular season, both to Cassie and the Orioles. Jack knew from having seen both games that they not only had as many good hitters as the Orioles did, they also had the second-best pitcher in their league, Karla Johnson.

But as good as Karla was and as good as the Dodgers were, Cassie was the show.

She was pitching in front of the biggest crowd the Orioles had had all season, and she was the one dealing tonight. She struck out the first two batters of the game, gave up a single, and struck out Karla on three pitches.

She struck out two more in the second, two more in the third. In the bottom of the third, she tripled up the alley in right-center, and Katie Cummings singled her home for the first run of the game.

Her dad had decided beforehand that she could pitch four innings tonight. It wasn't just that her pitch count was low, it was that it was the championship game. Before she went back out to the mound for the top of the fourth, she walked over to Jack and said, "You know I could go the distance tonight if I had to."

"No doubt."

"I feel awesome."

"You look awesome out there," Jack said. "Now just go out and pitch this inning like it's the last one you're ever going to pitch."

"Thanks, Coach," she said, and sprinted to get the ball.

She gave up another hit in the inning, and a walk, and Jack wondered if she could possibly have lost it that fast. But he watched as she walked behind the mound, rubbing up the ball as she looked at the base runners.

Then she looked at Jack, and she smiled, like she was exactly where she was supposed to be.

Then she proceeded to strike out the side. On nine pitches. The game stayed 1–0. There were no smiles now as she walked off the mound, no fist pumps. She just stared straight ahead, walked to the bench, placed her glove on it, grabbed her water bottle out of her bat bag, and took a swig.

When she finished doing that, she looked at Jack and winked.

Teddy and Gus were hanging over the fence. Jack went up to them and said, "How cool is she?"

"Pretty much the coolest," Gus said.

Teddy said to Jack, "I don't want to be you anymore. I think I want to be her."

"You know why?" Jack said. "Because the only thing she's afraid of is somebody else pitching the rest of the game."

"That somebody happens to be my sister," Gus said.

"No offense, dude."

"None taken." Gus laughed. "Because I'm scared too!"

"Angela will be fine," Jack said. "Her fear of blowing this

and having to deal with Cassie will be a great motivator."

Angela Morales got through a sketchy fifth, leaving two runners on. Cassie got her out of it by flashing behind second, getting her glove on what looked like a two-out single from the Dodgers' Emily Curley, making a sliding stop, and flipping the ball to Gracie Zaro for the third out.

It was still 1–0 when Angela and the Orioles got ready to take the field for the top of the sixth, three outs from the championship.

Cassie walked over to where Jack was standing and put out her fist. He touched it with his own.

"Only game," she said.

"Only one."

Angela got two quick outs, the best possible thing in a moment like this, for her and for all of them, giving them all some room to breathe. One out away.

But then the girl hitting ahead of Karla ripped a single over Gracie's head and proceeded to steal second, and then third. So the tying run was on third with Karla Johnson, their best hitter as well as their best pitcher, coming to the plate.

As much as Jack wanted Cassie to win, maybe this was the way a great game like this was supposed to end. The only thing that would have made it better, he thought, was if Cassie was still on the mound.

He found out he was wrong on the very next pitch.

Karla took a huge swing but topped the ball, rolling it toward short, the ball looking as if it were going to die in the infield grass before it got to Cassie.

Jack had the whole play in front of him, saw the runner coming down the line from third, saw Karla running hard with her head down toward first.

But then his eyes were on Cassie Bennett, barehanding the ball—hard to do with a softball—and whipping it sidearm across the diamond into Katie Cummings's outstretched first baseman's mitt.

One last time this season, Cassie was showing off the best arm in her league. Or maybe the best arm any girl her age had anywhere.

She threw one last fastball and got Karla by one step and won the championship game for the Orioles, 1–0.

And when the celebration was over on the field, when Cassie had hugged her teammates and her dad, she walked over to where Jack had watched from the sidelines. He knew it was where he belonged. He had been happy to be a part of her team, and its season. But this was their moment.

"You know where I learned how to do that?" she said.

"Where?"

"From watching you."

THE ONLY GAME

"I don't know that I could have made a play like that with it all on the line."

"Yeah," Cassie said. "Yeah, you would have."

Then she hugged him, too.

When they both came out of the hug, neither one wanting it to last too long, Cassie said, "Now it's your turn."

They both knew what she meant. Time to win two games and finish a season right that he nearly hadn't started.

THIRTY-
SIX

There was a half day of school at Walton Middle on Wednesday. It was just Walton being a baseball town because of the semifinals in the Atlantic later on.

With four teams playing, that was a lot of students from Walton Middle. Before they were all let out at noon, the principal came over the PA system and encouraged everybody to show up for the two games:

White Sox vs. Rangers at five thirty.

Rays vs. Mariners at seven thirty.

Before they left school, Jack told Teddy and Gus that he'd check them later, maybe they could meet up at his house and hang there before heading over to watch the first game of the doubleheader.

When Jack and Cassie were walking home, he asked if she was interested in watching the White Sox and the Rangers.

"Not even a little bit," she said. "It feels to me like the JV game."

"Wait a second," he said. "The White Sox just beat us last Saturday."

"You wouldn't have lost if it was the play-offs," she said. "You guys are winning tonight and then beating whoever wins the JV game on Saturday."

"You sound pretty sure."

"The only way I'd feel more sure," she said, "would be if I were playing." She gave him a little shove. "You know I could've replaced Scott at catcher, right?"

Jack grinned. "I actually thought about it. But I figured playing with boys was beneath you."

His mom fixed him a sandwich when he got home. When Jack finished eating, he went upstairs and tried to watch a movie, just to take his mind off the game, but knew he was wasting his time. He just wanted time to go fast. He wanted the afternoon to be over and the White Sox–Rangers game to be over and for their game to be starting. Instead time was standing still.

He finally grabbed his phone and shot Teddy a text.

ON MY WAY TO UR HOUSE, GOTTA GET OUT OF MINE,

FORGET EARLIER PLAN.

He didn't get a response right back, but that probably meant Teddy was having lunch with his mom, whom he'd said had taken a half day herself. She had a rule about him not having his phone at the table, doing what she called the "look down" when they were having a meal together.

Jack told his mom he'd be back in a couple of hours, then grabbed his bike and headed for Teddy's, taking his time, taking a longer route than he usually did. He felt like it was the end of a basketball game and he was taking time off the clock.

Mrs. Madden's car was in the driveway when he got there. He leaned his bike against their mailbox, walked up the steps, and rang the doorbell.

When she opened the door, Jack said, "Hey, Mrs. Madden. I'm looking for my catcher."

Jack could see right away that she was confused.

"But I thought he was with you, Jack."

"He was supposed to be later. But I couldn't sit around in my room any longer, so I decided to come over here just to have something to do."

"Well, my boy was acting all wound up himself," she said. "Then he went and got his bike and told me he had something to do, and then he was heading for your house."

"Did he say what he had to do?"

She shook her head. "No. But whatever it was, he made it sound important. I asked him what, and he said, 'It's just something I need to do before I can play the game tonight.' Said it was something he should have done a while ago if he wanted to be a real ballplayer. He left in such a hurry he didn't even take his phone with him."

"Maybe he's just riding around the way I was."

"Maybe so," she said. "He really was such a bundle of nerves."

Jack said he'd call Mrs. Madden when he caught up with Teddy.

He tried not to look like he was in a hurry getting back on his bike. But he was in a hurry. Because he didn't think Teddy was just riding around.

Jack thought Teddy had a destination.

No.

He didn't just *think* that.

Somehow he knew.

Knew in his heart that this time it might not be his brother being somewhere he shouldn't be. It was his friend.

When Jack was back on his bike, he rode fast. He wanted to be wrong. He kept hoping he was wrong all the way back across town. But when he saw Teddy's bike at the Connorses' dock, he knew he wasn't.

I feel like I'm back at the bridge, Teddy had said the other day.

Maybe he had to prove himself to himself. Maybe he thought if he could face down his greatest fear, the others would be easy. Jack wasn't smart enough to know exactly why Teddy was up there.

But he was.

Jack ran. He didn't know the trails as well as Cassie did. But he felt as if he was taking the most direct route, the one he thought they'd taken the day Teddy couldn't make it across. He moved in and out of shadows, feeling himself going uphill as he went, feeling the wind on his face. He'd noticed the breeze picking up on his bike.

When he could hear the water, he yelled Teddy's name.

No response.

"Teddy, you up here?"

Still nothing.

When he finally approached the clearing that first brought the falls and the bridge in sight, Jack heard him.

"Jack?"

Suddenly it didn't matter why Teddy had come up here. He sounded more frightened than ever, out there somewhere between the water and the sky.

THIRTY-SEVEN

Teddy Madden was halfway across the bridge, which was swaying even more than it usually did because the wind was blowing even harder up here.

He had turned himself to face Jack. He seemed to have a death grip with his right hand on the thick rope that served as a railing.

"Don't look down," Jack said.

But that was exactly what Teddy did as soon as Jack said it. He looked down at the falls, then back at Jack.

"I . . . I can't get back," he said.

In that moment Jack thought of his brother. Brad never had any fears to overcome. Teddy was the opposite. But he'd decided to test himself today, the way Brad was always testing himself.

"Yes, you can," Jack said.

He made himself smile, as if this was no big deal, as if they were behind Walton Middle throwing a ball around instead of facing each other high above Small Falls. "Piece of cake," he said.

Teddy looked down again, then back at Jack.

"I can't move," he said. "I thought if I could do this, everything else would get easier. But I can't."

"You can," Jack said. "It's the same advice my mom gave me after my brother died. You just gotta put one foot in front of the other."

Teddy wasn't crying, but he was close.

Jack said, "Teddy, the guy who was afraid of the bridge—you're not that guy anymore."

"Yeah, I am."

"You're not!" Jack said. "If you were, you wouldn't be here in the first place."

Jack hoped he was saying the right things, but he had no idea whether he was or not. Had no idea if Teddy was really hearing him.

But what he did know was this: Teddy had to do this himself.

"You didn't think you'd ever play ball, but you proved you could do that," Jack said. "You can do this."

"You always think I'm better than I really am!"

"Now *that* you do have wrong," Jack said. "I see you for who you really are. I saw that before you did yourself."

"I can't make it back!" Teddy shouted.

"You're not going to."

"What does that mean?"

"It means you're going to turn around now and do what you came here to do and make it to the other side."

They stood there now, like it was some kind of stare-down on the playground, neither one of them saying anything over the howl of the wind and the water.

"One foot in front of the other," Jack said. "Go on."

Maybe only Teddy knew how much effort it took to turn himself back around. Or take his first step away from Jack. But he did. He walked slowly. He stopped a couple more times. Every time he did, Jack thought that time really had stopped this afternoon.

But Teddy finally made it to the other side.

MIKE LUPICA

When he did, he turned and looked at Jack and gave a slight nod of his head. Like he was saying yes. Then he was nodding again and again. Yes, yes, yes.

Then it was Jack's turn. He didn't look down himself, and he wasn't very happy being out on this old bridge in a wind like this. He wasn't walking too quickly either. But he made it to the other side.

When he stepped off the bridge, Teddy said, "Thank you."

Jack shook his head.

"It's like I told you about baseball," he said. "You did this, not me."

Then they walked back across the bridge together, without stopping once.

THIRTY-EIGHT

The White Sox had already played their way into the championship game, winning 4–2. Now the Rays would try to do the same.

The plan was for Andre to pitch the first four innings, depending on his pitch count, and Jerry York to pitch the last two.

Because the Rays had finished second and the Mariners third, the Rays were the home team. Before they took the field, Coach Leonard led them down the rightfield line and then gathered his players around him. Jack was waiting for his teammates there. He'd been down there by himself, sitting by himself the way he always did before games. Tonight the quiet time seemed more important than ever.

"Don't do this for me tonight and don't do it for your parents," Coach said. "Find the best in yourselves tonight for yourselves. I'm not going to tell you to have fun the way I usually do, because if you can't have fun with a game like this, you need to find another hobby."

He turned in a slow circle as he spoke, so it felt as if he were talking to each one of them individually.

"It's nights like this you remember when you're my age," he said. "Now go make it one all of us will never forget."

They walked back to the bench to get their gloves. Jack looked up in the stands and waved to his parents. He closed his eyes and pictured his brother up there, pointing at him and smiling the way he always did. He touched his back pocket, where Brad's note was. Then he felt himself smiling too.

Teddy was next to him, adjusting the straps on his chest protector, making sure it wasn't too tight. He and Jack and Gus had watched the whole White Sox game together. Jack hadn't brought up what had happened earlier at Small Falls, and neither had Teddy.

"You good?" Jack said to him now.

Teddy said, "Let's do this."

Gus came walking over and put his first baseman's mitt in the air. Teddy tapped it with his catcher's mitt. Jack did the same with his Pedroia.

Gus turned to Jack and said, "Take us out."

Jack led Gus and Teddy and his teammates onto the field. It had been a long wait for the first pitch. But man, had it been worth it.

Teddy did throw out the first guy who tried to run on him. It was the Mariners' second baseman, Nick Tierney, who'd singled off Andre with two outs. The batter took the pitch, and Teddy came up throwing like a pro, giving Jack a perfect ball to handle at second. Jack put the tag on Nick. Before he ran off the field, he pointed at Teddy. Teddy, standing at the plate with his mask in his hand, pointed back at him. Game on.

But by the time they were in the bottom of the fifth, the Mariners had just scored three times off Jerry to take a 5–3 lead. Gregg Leonard nearly made an unbelievable diving play with two outs and the bases loaded. But he couldn't quite get to the ball before it hit the ground. The ball rolled behind him, and three guys scored. The Mariners were up two. Two at bats left for the Rays, maybe in their season.

It looked as if the score would stay that way in the bottom of the fifth when there were two outs and nobody on. But then Andre singled between first and second, and Jerry, who'd just given up that triple, doubled him to third.

Teddy came to the plate. He was 0 for 2 on the night and had struck out twice, even though he had played his best game behind the plate so far. He had thrown out another base stealer, nearly gotten another. He'd also made a terrific diving play on a bunt, laying out as he caught the ball in the air, throwing to Gus from his knees to get a double play.

Let him get a hit, Jack thought. *Let him prove to himself that he can do that, too.*

Nick Tierney was on the mound for the Mariners, having moved in from second. His first pitch to Teddy knifed down and bounced off home plate. Teddy swung at it anyway.

Then he swung through the next one, a belt-high fastball.

With an 0–2 count, wanting the strikeout right here, Nick threw the same pitch again. Teddy barely got a piece of it but stayed alive when their catcher couldn't hold the foul tip. Teddy stepped out and banged his helmet with his right hand. He'd missed another good pitch and knew it.

Jack was seated next to Gus on the bench.

"Wait," he said in a low voice.

Gus nodded. Nick came to the stretch. This fastball was still belt high, but a little more inside than the last two. Teddy waited on this one.

When his new Easton bat came through the hitting zone, he

was all over it, lining a single over shortstop. With two outs, Jerry was running as soon as the ball was hit, rounding third as if he were trying to catch Andre at home plate, Coach Leonard waving him home. Their leftfielder threw home. It wasn't even close. Jerry slid across the plate, and the game was tied.

Two-out, two-run hit for Teddy.

T.W. struck out to end the fifth. When Teddy came off the field, he ran quickly through the high fives from his teammates, sat down, and started strapping on his shin guards.

"You can at least look happy," Jack said.

"We've got more work to do," Teddy said.

"You sound like a player."

"Yeah," Teddy said, "I do, don't I?"

Then he allowed himself one smile and said to Jack, "Second-best thing I did all day."

The Mariners came right back. They had runners on first and third against Jerry with two outs. Their third baseman, Jake Mosedean, was at the plate. Max Conte was on third.

With the count 0–1 on Jake, they tried a double steal you saw a lot in Little League. The runner on first took off for second, and the runner on third took off for home as soon as the catcher released the ball. It worked a lot if the catcher didn't know enough to hold the ball.

As soon as Teddy came out of his crouch and came up

throwing, Max headed home.

Only Teddy didn't throw. Not only did he fake out the runners with the kind of pump fake quarterbacks made in football, he faked out Jack, who was already putting down his glove at second base.

But the ball was still in his hand. Max was about ten feet away from the plate when Teddy turned and ran at him. Max had no chance to turn around and try to get into a rundown; he just stood there while Teddy put the tag on him.

The game stayed 5–5, just not for very long.

Gregg led off the bottom of the last with a bloop hit that landed a few feet fair down the rightfield line, and he legged that into an easy double. Nick pitched too carefully to Jack and walked him. Gus Morales then hit the first pitch he saw from Nick off the leftfield wall, missing a three-run walk-off homer by about three feet. Gregg Leonard ran home with the winning run. Jack looked behind him and saw Gus's right arm in the air as he came around first. They were in the championship game.

They all mobbed Gus between first and second. Then Jack grabbed Teddy by the shoulders.

"I never taught you to hold the ball like that on a double steal," he said.

"Nope," Teddy said. "Some things you just gotta figure out for yourself, right?"

THIRTY-NINE

The championship game on Saturday night was scheduled for seven o'clock. It was another big Walton baseball game, under the lights. But it was also another long day of waiting.

Jack and Gus and Teddy and Cassie had spent the day together, Cassie acting as intense about the game as if she were playing it. They went to Fierro's for lunch, then to Baskin-Robbins for ice cream, then back to Jack's house for Wiffle ball.

Teddy and Gus finally left, telling Jack they'd see him at

Highland Park at five thirty. As Cassie was leaving, she asked if his parents could pick her up on their way to the field.

"Hey," she said, "I'm not missing any of this."

"I wouldn't have even made it this far without you," Jack said.

"I hate to admit it," Cassie said, "but you're absolutely right."

When he was in his uniform an hour later, everything on except his baseball shoes, ready to go, he went and sat on the end of his brother's bed.

It was more quiet than quiet in here, as always. Jack thought of all the time in his life he'd spent in here when his brother was alive. Remembered all the goofy videos Brad just had to show him on YouTube as soon as he'd seen them himself. He remembered all the card tricks Brad had shown him, because Jack was his best audience.

Jack thought about all the times Brad had closed his door and lowered his voice and told Jack about his latest adventure. Or misadventure. Or planned his next one.

What he mostly remembered, in the quiet, was how much they'd laughed in here, just the two of them, even when Jack was nervous before a game.

"Figured we might find you in here," his dad said.

Jack looked up. Both his parents were standing in the doorway, his dad's arm around his mother's shoulders.

"I was just thinking of all the things he used to say to get me ready for the game."

"He would have had more fun than anybody tonight," his dad said.

Jack grinned. "Except me."

"Except you," his mom said.

"He wrote in his letter that he loved us the way I love baseball," Jack said. "But I loved him more."

"And he knew that," his mom said.

Jack stood up. His parents walked across the room. They all hugged in the middle of the room. Nobody cried this time. When they pulled out of the hug, Jack could see both his parents smiling.

"You ready?" his dad said.

"Oh yeah."

He went back to his own room, grabbed his bat bag off his bed, rubbed up his Pedroia ball one last time for luck, then went to play the big game.

Five minutes before the game, the stands on both side of the field were full. They'd just played the national anthem over the loudspeakers. The White Sox were on the field. Jack was sitting between Gus and Teddy on their bench, on the third-base side tonight, because the White Sox were the home team.

"Number one against number two," Jack said. "I guess that's the way it's supposed to be."

"There's only one 'one' here tonight," Gus said. "That would be us."

"If you think about it," Teddy said, "even if Jack had started the season, it would probably be us against the White Sox. We'd just be sitting on the other side of the field."

"We lost to them once," Gus said. "Not happening again."

"I'm just glad to get another chance at these guys," Jack said.

Teddy asked if Jack wanted to throw a few more warm-up pitches behind the bench.

"I'm good," Jack said.

"Me too," Teddy said. "Tonight I've got those good nerves you're always talking about going for me."

Coach Leonard came over and stood in front of all of them. He'd already spoken to them in the outfield, the way he always did, quoting from what he said was his favorite sports movie, *Miracle*, about the US hockey team that won the gold medal in Lake Placid, upsetting the Russians along the way.

"This is your time," Coach had told them.

Now all he said was, "As long as we're here, let's go win a championship."

He looked around. "Anything anybody wants to add?"

Gus stood up and put his right hand in the air. His teammates got around him and put their own hands up to join his. "Go Rays," Gus said.

As T.W. got ready to lead off the top of the first, Jack and Gus had already put their batting helmets on, already grabbed their bats. They were standing behind the bench.

"I only got mad at you because I didn't want to do this without you," Gus said.

"I'm glad you didn't have to."

Gus said, "If we win tonight, you know nobody's going to stop us this summer on the way to Williamsport."

"Let's just win tonight."

Gus grinned. "If you say so."

Jack turned and took one last look around, gave one last wave to his parents. He looked down the leftfield line and saw Cassie's head peeking around the ice cream truck parked behind the fence. He touched Brad's note one last time, thinking of the part in it about how someday he was going to watch Jack play at Fenway Park or Yankee Stadium.

But that wasn't the dream tonight.

Tonight the dream was here.

FORTY

Nate Vinton had his best stuff going for the White Sox, the
same as he had the last time he'd faced the Rays, until
they'd finally gotten to him in the last inning he'd pitched.

The only run scored by either team in the first four innings
came in the top of the first, two outs for the Rays and nobody
on. Jack doubled to left-center, Gus walked, Brett Hawkins
singled home Jack.

Coach always talked about getting the first strike, the first out, the first run. Baseball was a game of firsts, he said. The Rays were on the scoreboard first, even if Nate kept them off it after that.

But Jack was better tonight. He walked Wayne Coffey with one out in the first. He'd end up walking Wayne again on a very close 3–2 pitch in the third. Those were the only two base runners in his four innings on the mound. He struck out eight batters.

From the start, working out with Teddy, he'd always talked about the two of them just playing catch. That was the way it felt for him in the championship game. This was what you always hoped for in sports, playing your best when the games mattered the most.

Biggest game.

Best game.

Only game.

When he came back to the bench after he'd finished off the bottom of the fourth with his last two strikeouts, Gus said, "We need a better word than 'dealing' for what I just saw."

"What we need," Jack said, "is a run."

Teddy said, "Our game can't end 1–0 the way Cassie's did, right?"

"Unlikely," Gus said, "with the two studs out of the game. This could get good now."

"It's not good already?" Teddy said.

"He meant it could get better than it already is," Jack said.

The Rays couldn't score off the White Sox's best reliever, Danny Hayes, in the top of the fifth, going down in order.

Jerry was pitching for the Rays now. He got two quick outs in the bottom of the fifth and seemed to be breezing. But then Hawk booted an easy ball hit by Nate that would have given Jerry an easy inning, and the whole thing became a mess after that. Nate got a great jump and stole second, even though Teddy made a sweet throw and nearly got him.

Mike O'Keeffe singled home Nate. The game was tied. Danny doubled home Mike. The White Sox were ahead 2–1. Jerry walked two guys after that but managed to keep it a one-run game. Coach Leonard always talked about how fast the story changed in sports. The story in the championship game had changed that fast.

They had gone from being six outs away from the trophy to three outs away from going home, maybe just one inning left in their season.

It was why, when they got back to the bench, Jack told his teammates to gather around him. He'd never done anything like this in a game before, not one time since he'd started playing baseball. But it just seemed as if he needed to say something. He remembered Dustin Pedroia's teammate, David

Ortiz, doing it one time when the Red Sox were playing the Cardinals in the World Series and things were starting to look bad for the Red Sox.

"We're the best team in this league, and we're going to be the best team now," he said.

He was the one looking into one face after another, not Coach Leonard.

"You know I never make speeches," Jack said. "But we've come too far to lose now."

Teddy led off the top of the sixth with a clean single to left. It was a good thing, obviously, getting the leadoff man on. But as slow a runner as Teddy was, a lot was going to have to happen to get him around the bases.

T.W. struck out.

Gregg hit the ball harder than he had all night, but right at Conor Freeman at short.

Jack walked to the plate. If he couldn't get on, the season was over. If he couldn't do something right now, he was going to lose in the championship game for the second year in a row. After coming this far.

Before he'd left the on-deck circle, he'd knelt down and put some dirt in his hands, rubbed the dirt on his bat handle. As he did, he looked to the top row of the stands. He saw his dad and mom up there.

And in that moment, his brother, too.

"Game on the line, little bro?" he used to say to Jack. "Nobody else I'd ever want up there except you."

Game on the line here. Season on the line.

He took a strike, on the inside corner.

Then Danny threw him two balls, both inside as well. Maybe he knew what everybody else in their league knew, how hard and how far Jack could hit the ball to rightfield; how that was his real power.

If you're ever going to wait, Jack told himself, *wait now.*

He wasn't just waiting with his hands, and with his swing. He was telling himself to wait for his pitch. And got it from Danny. And got just underneath it enough to foul it back.

Shoot, shoot, shoot.

From the time he'd started playing ball, everything always seemed to get quiet for him in moments like this. Even though he'd never had a moment quite like this.

Danny Hayes tried to come inside again. But the ball ended up over the outside corner. The outer half, that's what the announcers liked to say.

Jack tried to hit the ball into outer space.

Maybe nobody else at Highland Park knew for sure that the ball was gone when they saw it heading high and deep toward the rightfield wall. Jack knew.

He came flying out of the box and toward first, but he knew, only slowing down when the ball cleared the fence by as much as it did. One of those homers you always dreamed about hitting in baseball, the kind that you hoped wouldn't stop rolling even when the game was over.

This one wasn't over yet, not by a long shot. But it was 3–2 Rays at Highland Park.

Gus tried to make it 4–2 three pitches later, but Wayne Coffey caught up with Gus's try for a homer about a yard short of the wall in dead center.

They were still up by a run going to the bottom of the sixth, maybe the bottom of the last.

Before they took the field, Gus grabbed Jack and said, "Any more words of inspiration from the home run king?"

Jack turned to Teddy. "You tell him."

"Little more work to do," Teddy said.

Turned out to be a lot.

FORTY-ONE

t came down to the White Sox's best player, Nate Vinton, up with a chance to be a hero in the bottom of the sixth. It was Nate who was going to be the hero or the last out for his team, with both the potential tying run and championship run on base.

Conor Freeman on second.

Wayne on first.

A 2–2 count on Nate.

He was the one down to his last strike when he was able to muscle a ball just between Gus and T.W. and toward Andre Williams, who had moved over to rightfield when Jerry came in to pitch.

Two things happened next, both huge.

Conor stumbled between second and third in his haste to get home with the tying run, and nearly went down.

That was one.

Two? Andre Williams got an amazing jump on the ball, charging it and picking it up in short right and coming up throwing as Conor finally got around third and headed for home.

The only problem was that in Andre's haste to make a strong throw to the plate, he slipped slightly, his throw ballooning toward the infield. Everybody could see it was going to come up way short, near the pitcher's mound instead of home plate. And neither Gus nor T.W. was there to be the cutoff man, because both of them had laid out trying to keep Nate's hit in the infield.

There was no cutoff man in sight until Jack was.

He was running at full speed from his position on the other side of the infield, at shortstop, the way Derek Jeter had one time in the play-offs, when he came out of nowhere to take a throw from the outfield and make one of the most famous defensive plays in history, a flip throw to the plate that saved a game for the

Yankees. Jack had watched the play a lot on YouTube. His dad had always said it was the best example he could ever remember in baseball of a player being in the right place at the right time.

Jack was in the right place now, catching up with Andre's throw, catching the ball in stride, gloving the ball and getting it in his throwing hand and making his own flip throw toward home plate without looking.

Toward Teddy.

Then Teddy was the one catching the ball in Scott Sutter's old mitt, making a sweep tag as Conor went into his slide, a good, hard, clean baseball slide.

He kicked up all this dirt.

Teddy kicked up his spikes as he went over on his back.

More dust and dirt from him.

When it cleared, Teddy was showing the home-plate ump that the ball was in the pocket of his mitt and Conor was out and the Rays were champions of the Atlantic.

In the next moment Jack was down there in the dirt with Teddy, and then the rest of the Rays were piling on top of them.

When they finally got to their feet, what felt like about an hour later, Teddy looked at Jack, smiling, face full of dirt and uniform full of dirt.

"Dude," he said. "You never told me the last step was the hardest."

THE ONLY GAME

FORTY-TWO

They were still at Highland Park an hour after the championship trophy had been presented in a ceremony at home plate. They had taken all the team pictures, before Coach Leonard leaned in and said to Jack, "I never thought I'd see that play again in my life. And never from a twelve-year-old."

Jack told him what his dad had said about being in the right place at the right time.

Coach put out his hand and said, "I'm happy for you."

Jack shook Coach's hand and said, "I'm happy for all of us."

"By the way? Turned out your catcher could catch."

Jack grinned. "Right place, right time," he said.

They both laughed.

Jack's mom and dad were sitting at the end of the Rays' bench, taking it all in. Cassie was with them. Jack walked over.

Cassie said, "The Jeter play? Seriously?"

Jack shrugged. "Just glad I thought of it before you did. And, Cass? That sidearm throw you made at the end of your game was harder."

"Shut up," she said, and then told him she needed one last slice of pizza. She walked over to the screen behind home plate where Mrs. Morales was passing them out.

It was Jack's mom who spoke next. For all of them.

"He would've loved it more than anyone," she said.

"The way he loved you," his dad said. "He'd be bragging about you all over the place, telling everybody that his little bro came up bigger than he ever had."

"And then," Jack said, "he would've been busting my chops as soon as we got home."

Jack looked over and saw Teddy near third base, posing for his mom as she took one more picture of him next to Coach and the championship trophy. When he broke loose, he and Gus met Jack near the pitcher's mound.

"You were there for me," Jack said to Teddy.

"Owed you one."

Jack said, "I owe you a lot more than you owe me."

"Got a question," Teddy said. "How do we ever top this?"

"Are you kidding?" Jack said. "We're just getting started. We're not even close to summer yet."

Teddy groaned.

"I'm not going to get much of a summer vacation, am I?" he said.

Jack and Gus looked at each other, then back at him, shaking their heads.

"We're going right back to work, aren't we?" Teddy said.

"No," Gus said. "Actually, we're going all the way to Williamsport."

And they did.